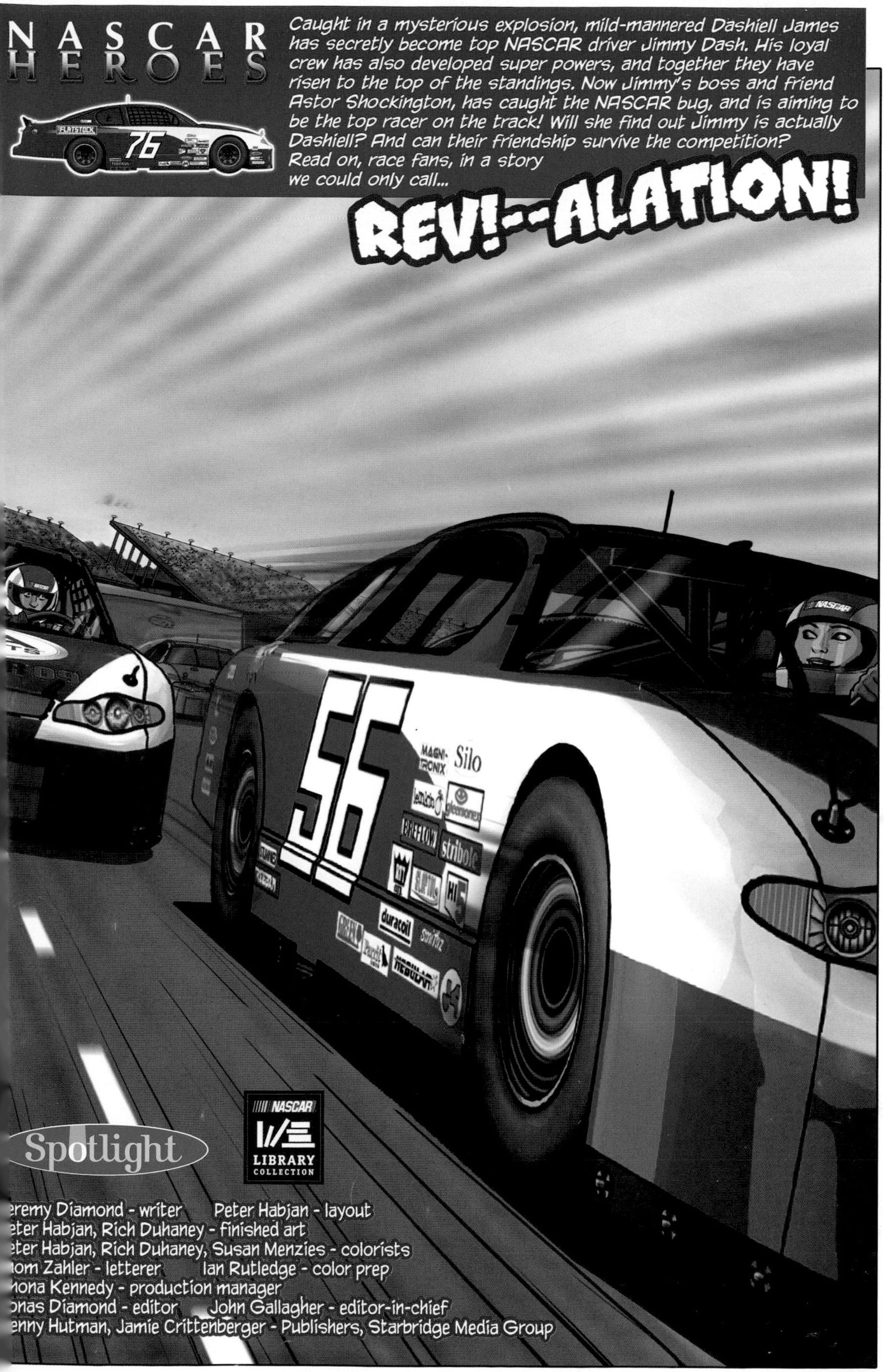
NASCAR HEROES
76
FLATSTOCK
Caught in a mysterious explosion, mild-mannered Dashiell James has secretly become top NASCAR driver Jimmy Dash. His loyal crew has also developed super powers, and together they have risen to the top of the standings. Now Jimmy's boss and friend Astor Shockington, has caught the NASCAR bug, and is aiming to be the top racer on the track! Will she find out Jimmy is actually Dashiell? And can their friendship survive the competition? Read on, race fans, in a story we could only call...
REV!--ALATION!
NASCAR
56
MAGNI-TRONIX
Silo
duracoil
Spotlight
NASCAR LIBRARY COLLECTION

eremy Diamond - writer Peter Habjan - layout
eter Habjan, Rich Duhaney - finished art
eter Habjan, Rich Duhaney, Susan Menzies - colorists
om Zahler - letterer Ian Rutledge - color prep
ona Kennedy - production manager
onas Diamond - editor John Gallagher - editor-in-chief
enny Hutman, Jamie Crittenberger - Publishers, Starbridge Media Group

VISIT US AT
www.abdopublishing.com

Reinforced library bound edition published in 2010 by Spotlight, a division of the ABDO Group, 800(West 78th Street, Edina, Minnesota 55439. Spotlight produces high-quality reinforced library bound editions for schools and libraries. Published by agreement with Starbridge Media Group, Inc.

Library of Congress Cataloging-in-Publication Data

Diamond, Jeremy.
Rev!-alation! / Jeremy Diamond, writer ; Peter Habjan, Rich Duhaney, finished art. -- Reinforced library bound ed.
p. cm. -- (NASCAR heroes ; #6)
"Nascar Library Collection."
Summary: When Astor begins driving Team Flatstock's second car, she and Jimmy Dash work agai one another, but their crew makes a great team as they try to break into archrival Diesel's trailer to ge sample of the substance that gave them all superpowers.
ISBN 978-1-59961-667-4
1. Graphic novels. [1. Graphic novels. 2. Automobile racing--Fiction. 3. NASCAR (Association)--Fiction. 4. Superheroes--Fiction.] I. Habjan, Peter, ill. II. Duhaney, Rich, ill. III. Title. IV. Title: Revelation!
PZ7.7.D52Rev 2009
741.5'973--dc22

2009009012

Spotlight

All Spotlight books have reinforced library bindings and are manufactured in the United States of

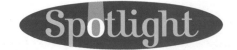

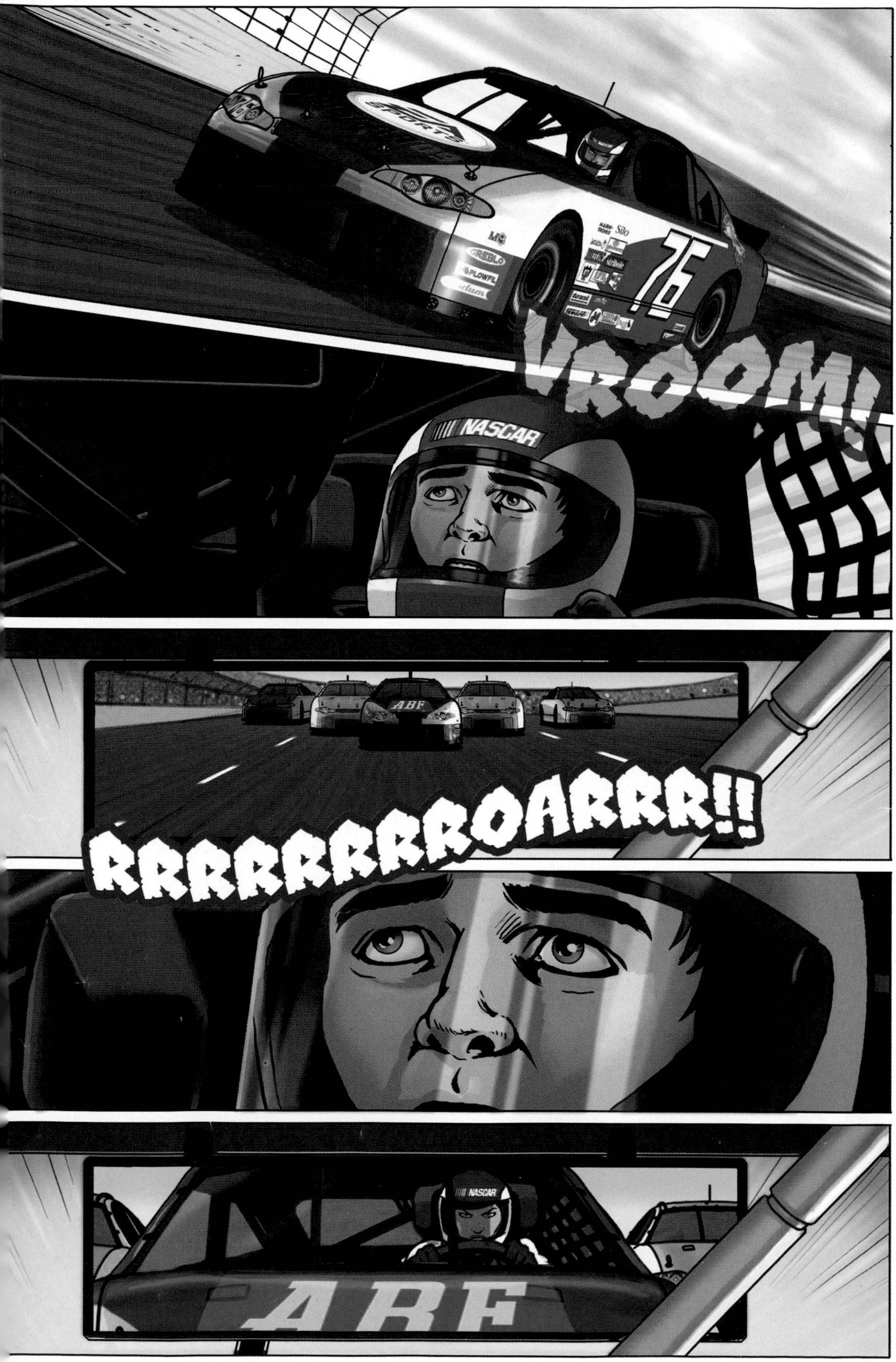

76
VROOM!
NASCAR
ABF
RRRRRRRROARRRR!!
NASCAR
ABF

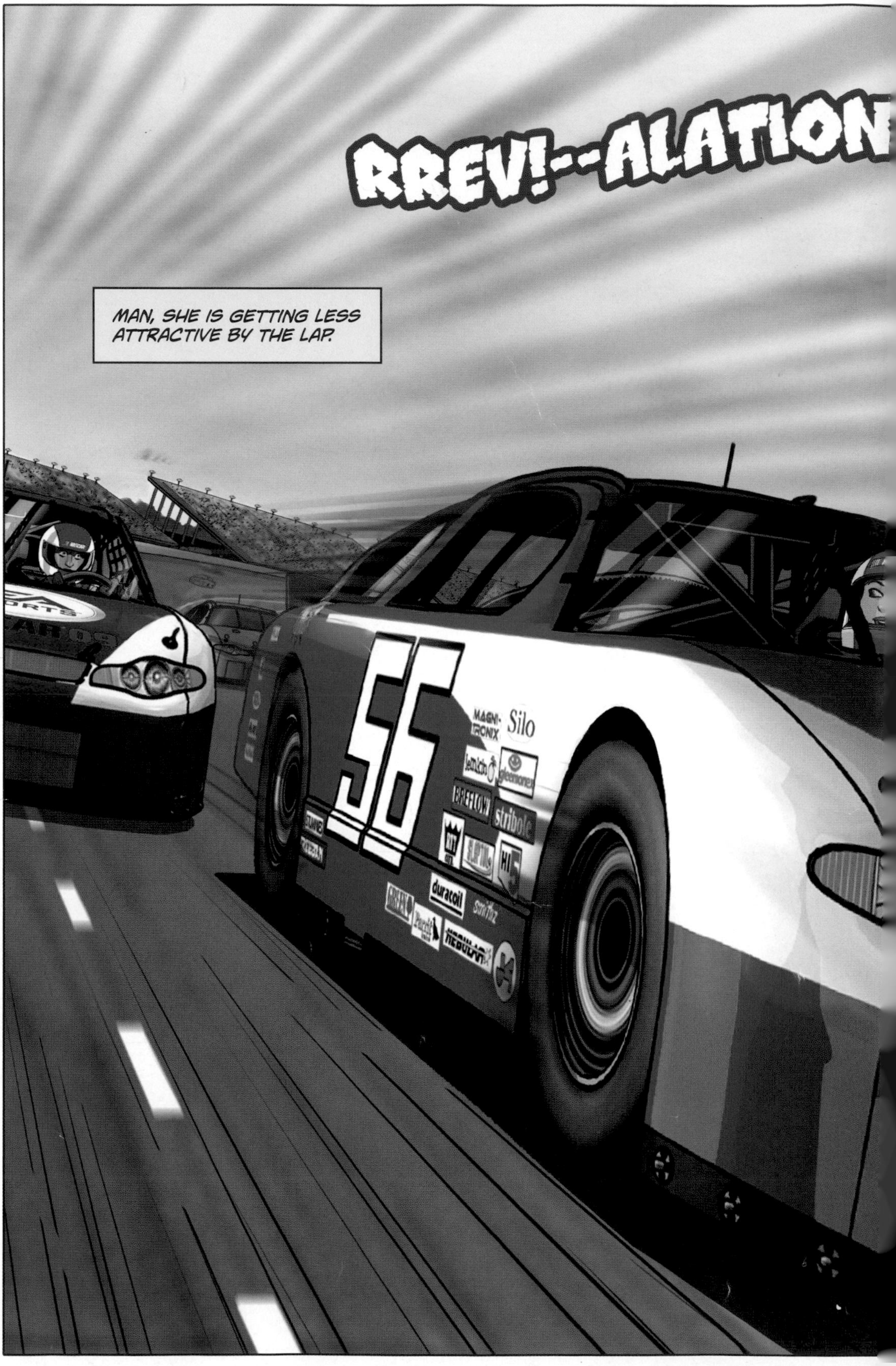
RREV!--ALATION
MAN, SHE IS GETTING LESS ATTRACTIVE BY THE LAP.
56

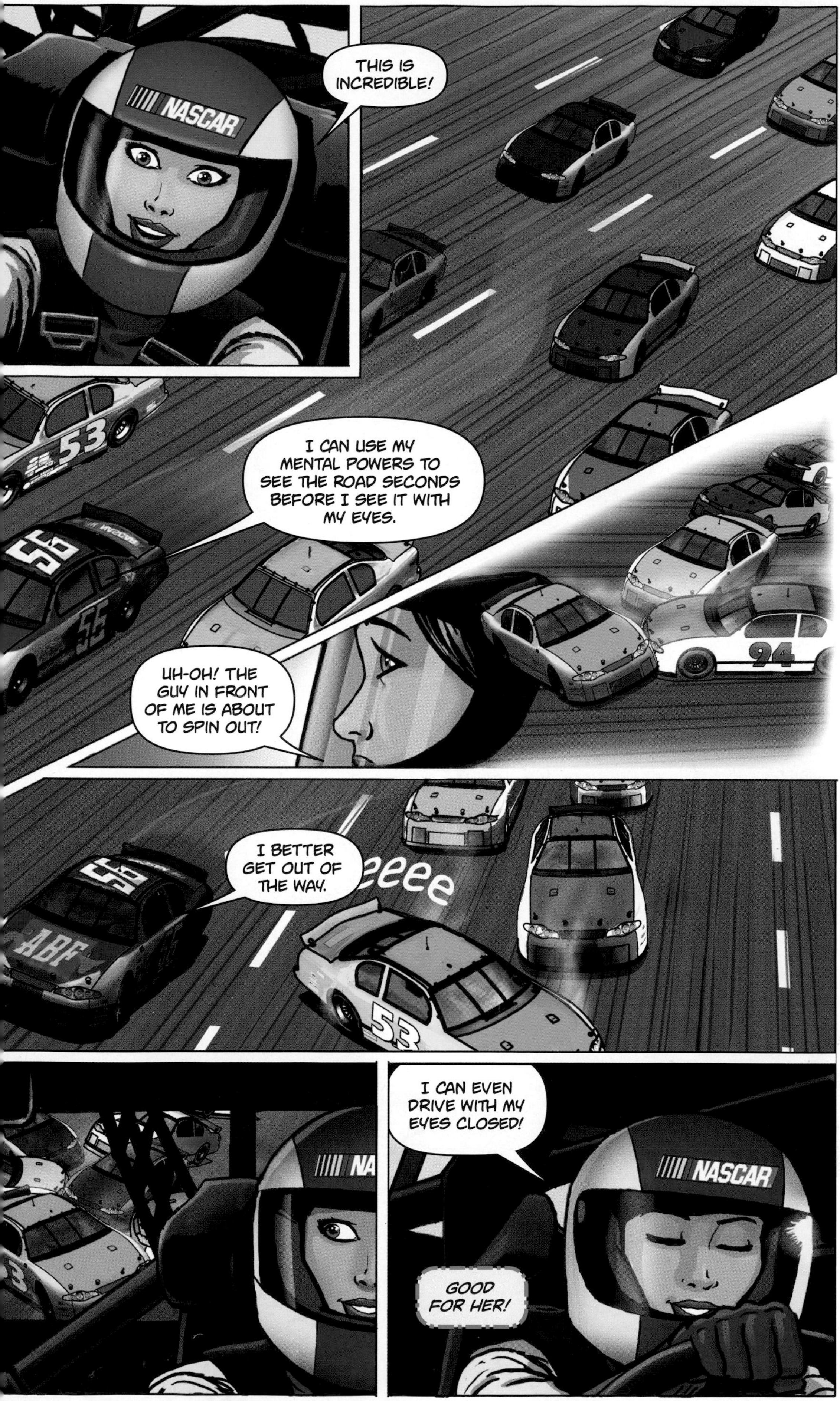
NASCAR
THIS IS INCREDIBLE!
53
I CAN USE MY MENTAL POWERS TO SEE THE ROAD SECONDS BEFORE I SEE IT WITH MY EYES.
55
UH-OH! THE GUY IN FRONT OF ME IS ABOUT TO SPIN OUT!
94
I BETTER GET OUT OF THE WAY.
eeee
ABF
53
I CAN EVEN DRIVE WITH MY EYES CLOSED!
NASCAR
GOOD FOR HER!

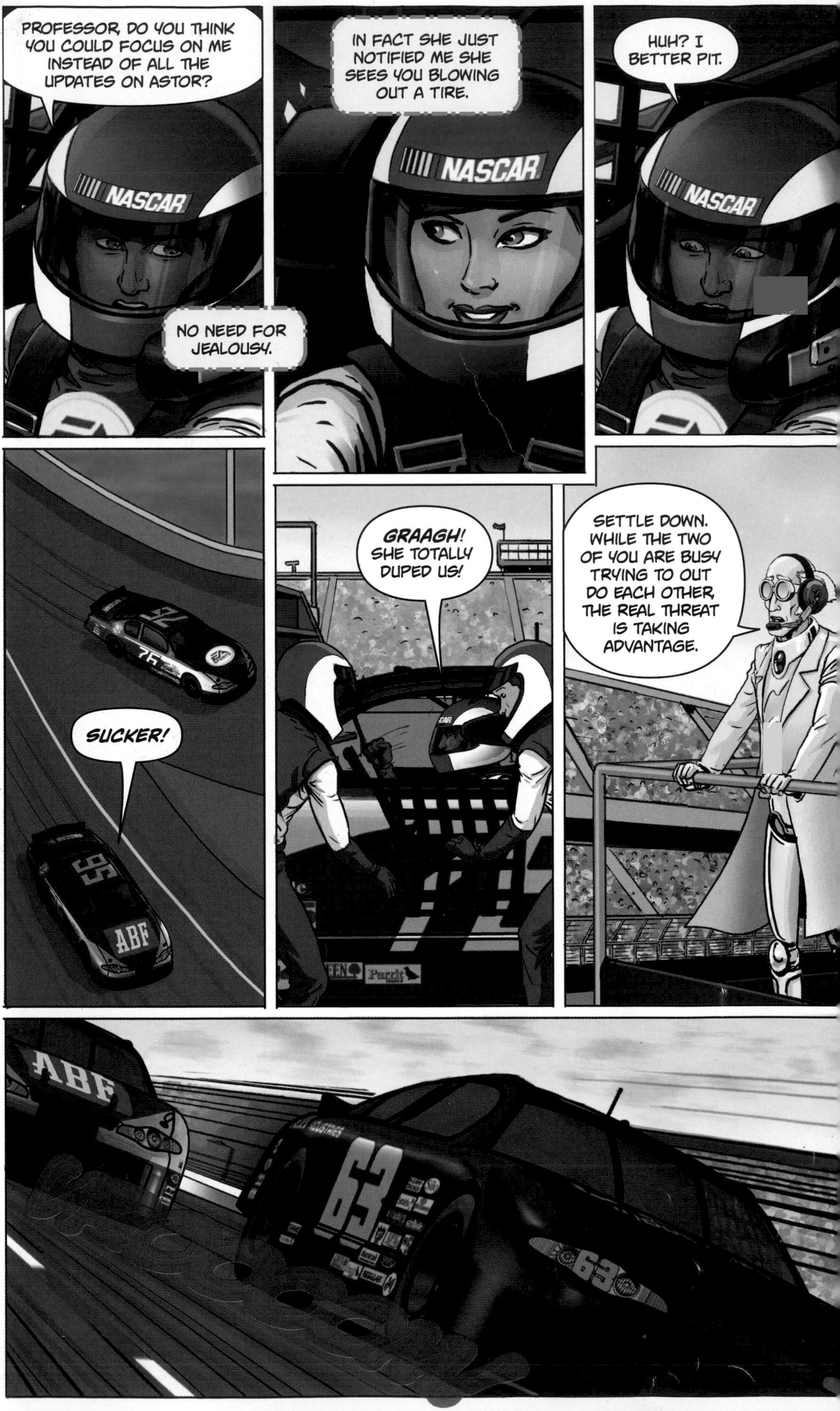
PROFESSOR, DO YOU THINK YOU COULD FOCUS ON ME INSTEAD OF ALL THE UPDATES ON ASTOR?
NO NEED FOR JEALOUSY.
IN FACT SHE JUST NOTIFIED ME SHE SEES YOU BLOWING OUT A TIRE.
HUH? I BETTER PIT.
SUCKER!
GRAAGH! SHE TOTALLY DUPED US!
SETTLE DOWN. WHILE THE TWO OF YOU ARE BUSY TRYING TO OUT DO EACH OTHER, THE REAL THREAT IS TAKING ADVANTAGE.

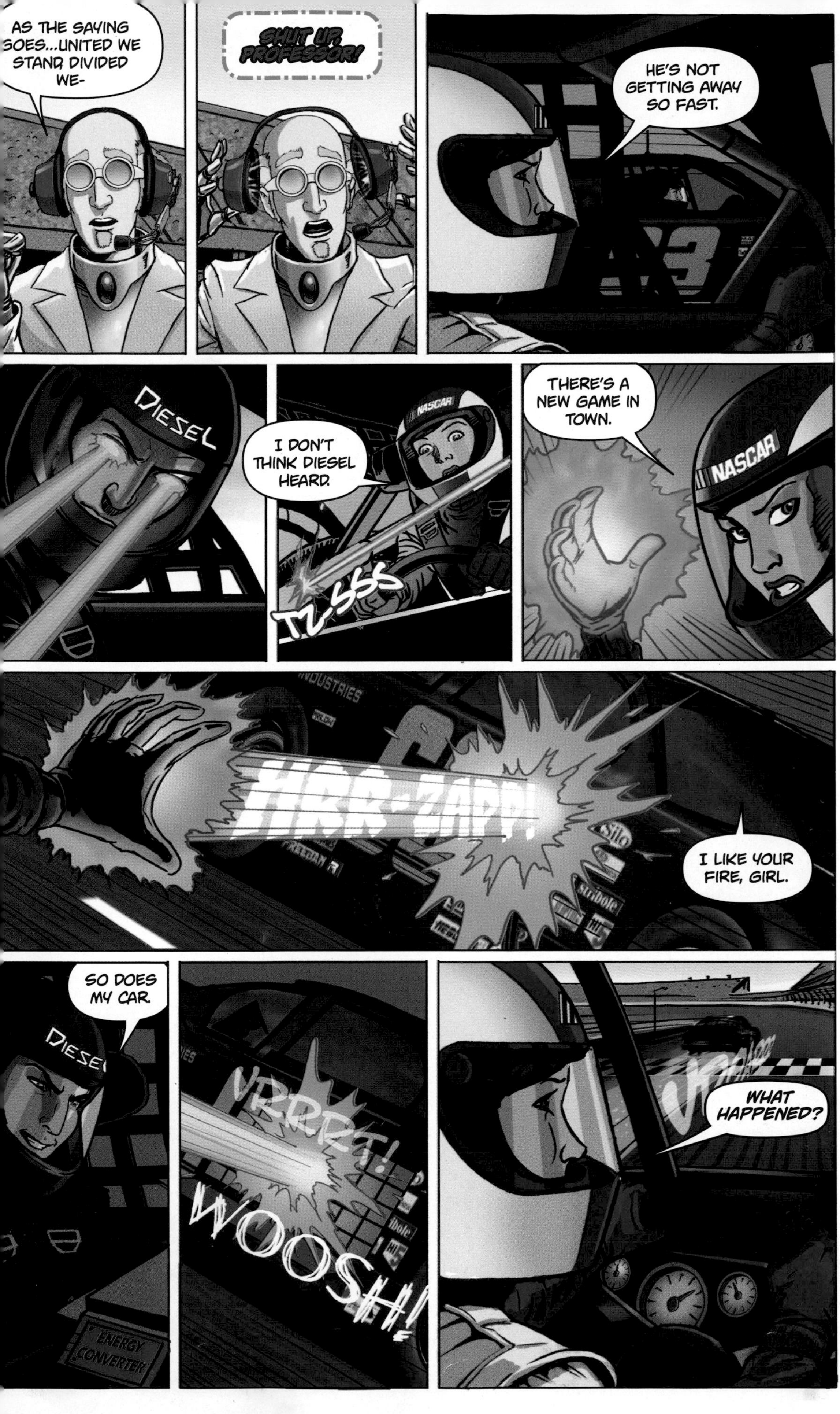
AS THE SAYING GOES...UNITED WE STAND, DIVIDED WE-
SHUT UP, PROFESSOR!
HE'S NOT GETTING AWAY SO FAST.
DIESEL
NASCAR
I DON'T THINK DIESEL HEARD.
TZ-SSS
THERE'S A NEW GAME IN TOWN.
NASCAR
HRR-ZAPP!
I LIKE YOUR FIRE, GIRL.
SO DOES MY CAR.
VRRRT!
WOOSH!
ENERGY CONVERTER
WHAT HAPPENED?

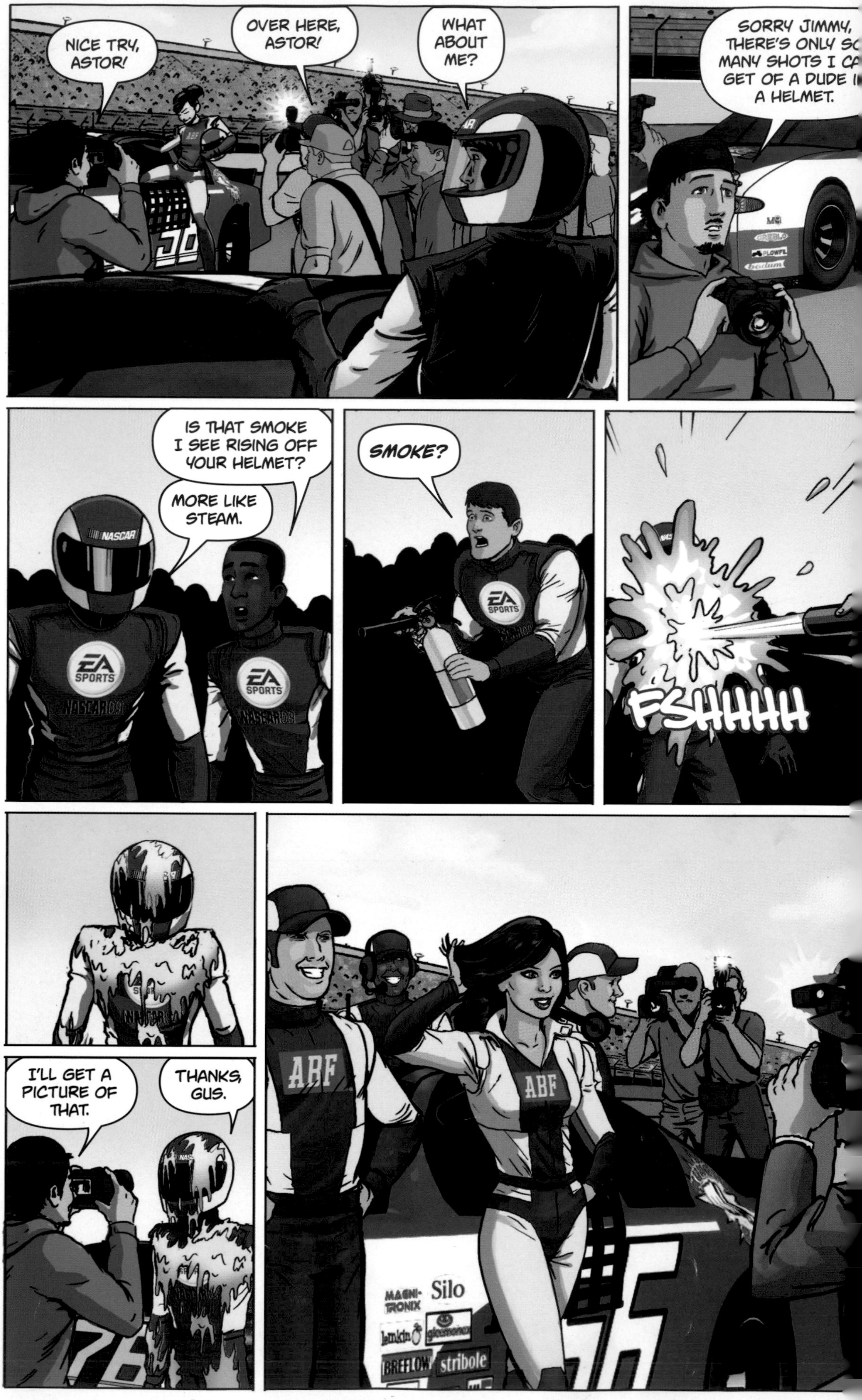
NICE TRY, ASTOR!
OVER HERE, ASTOR!
WHAT ABOUT ME?
SORRY JIMMY, THERE'S ONLY S MANY SHOTS I CA GET OF A DUDE I A HELMET.
IS THAT SMOKE I SEE RISING OFF YOUR HELMET?
MORE LIKE STEAM.
SMOKE?
FSHHHH
I'LL GET A PICTURE OF THAT.
THANKS, GUS.

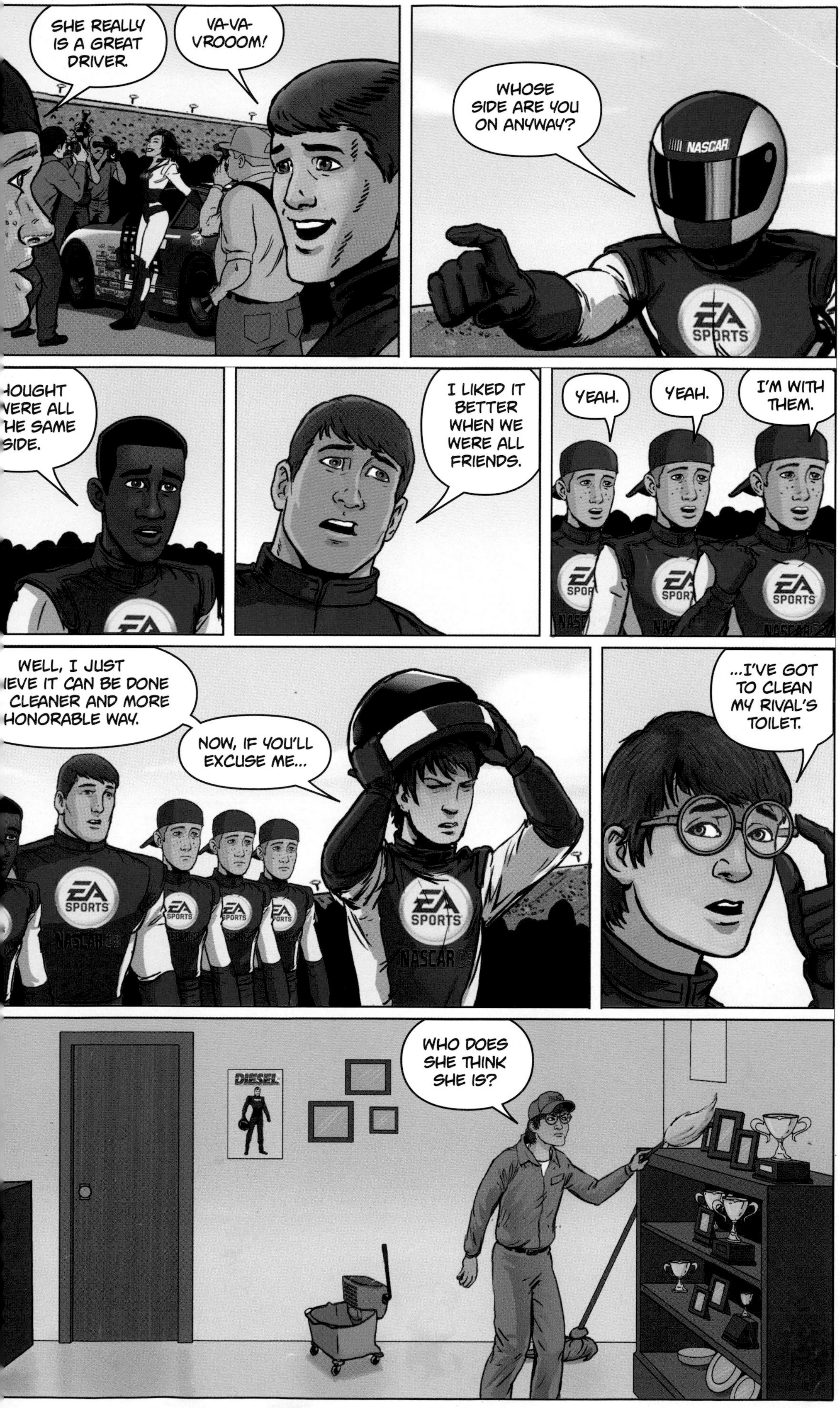
SHE REALLY IS A GREAT DRIVER.
VA-VA-VROOOM!
WHOSE SIDE ARE YOU ON ANYWAY?
NASCAR
EA SPORTS
HOUGHT VERE ALL HE SAME SIDE.
I LIKED IT BETTER WHEN WE WERE ALL FRIENDS.
YEAH.
YEAH.
I'M WITH THEM.
WELL, I JUST IEVE IT CAN BE DONE CLEANER AND MORE HONORABLE WAY.
NOW, IF YOU'LL EXCUSE ME...
...I'VE GOT TO CLEAN MY RIVAL'S TOILET.
DIESEL
WHO DOES SHE THINK SHE IS?

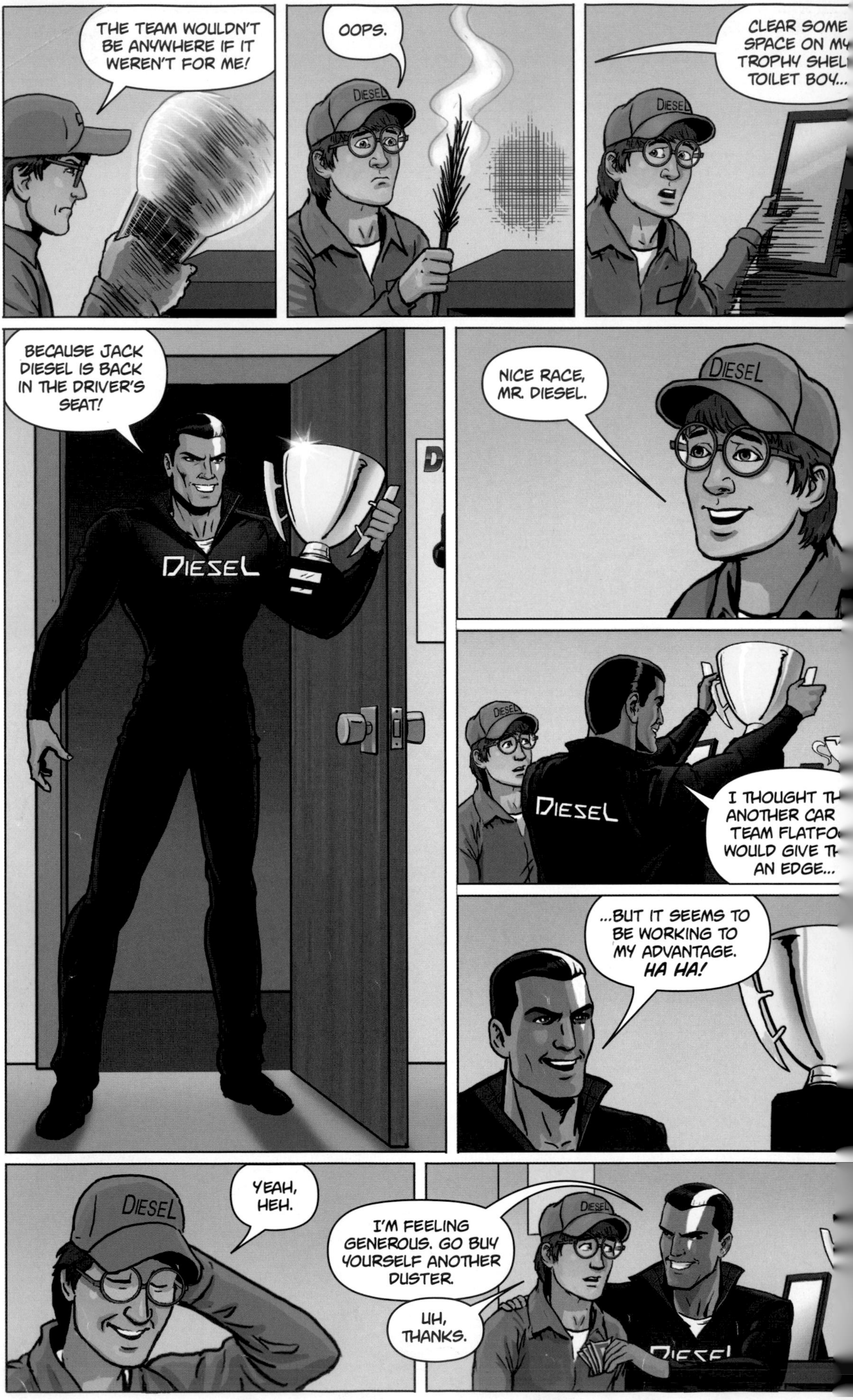
THE TEAM WOULDN'T BE ANYWHERE IF IT WEREN'T FOR ME!
OOPS.
CLEAR SOME SPACE ON MY TROPHY SHEL TOILET BOY...
BECAUSE JACK DIESEL IS BACK IN THE DRIVER'S SEAT!
NICE RACE, MR. DIESEL.
I THOUGHT TH ANOTHER CAR TEAM FLATFO WOULD GIVE TH AN EDGE...
...BUT IT SEEMS TO BE WORKING TO MY ADVANTAGE. *HA HA!*
YEAH, HEH.
I'M FEELING GENEROUS. GO BUY YOURSELF ANOTHER DUSTER.
UH, THANKS.

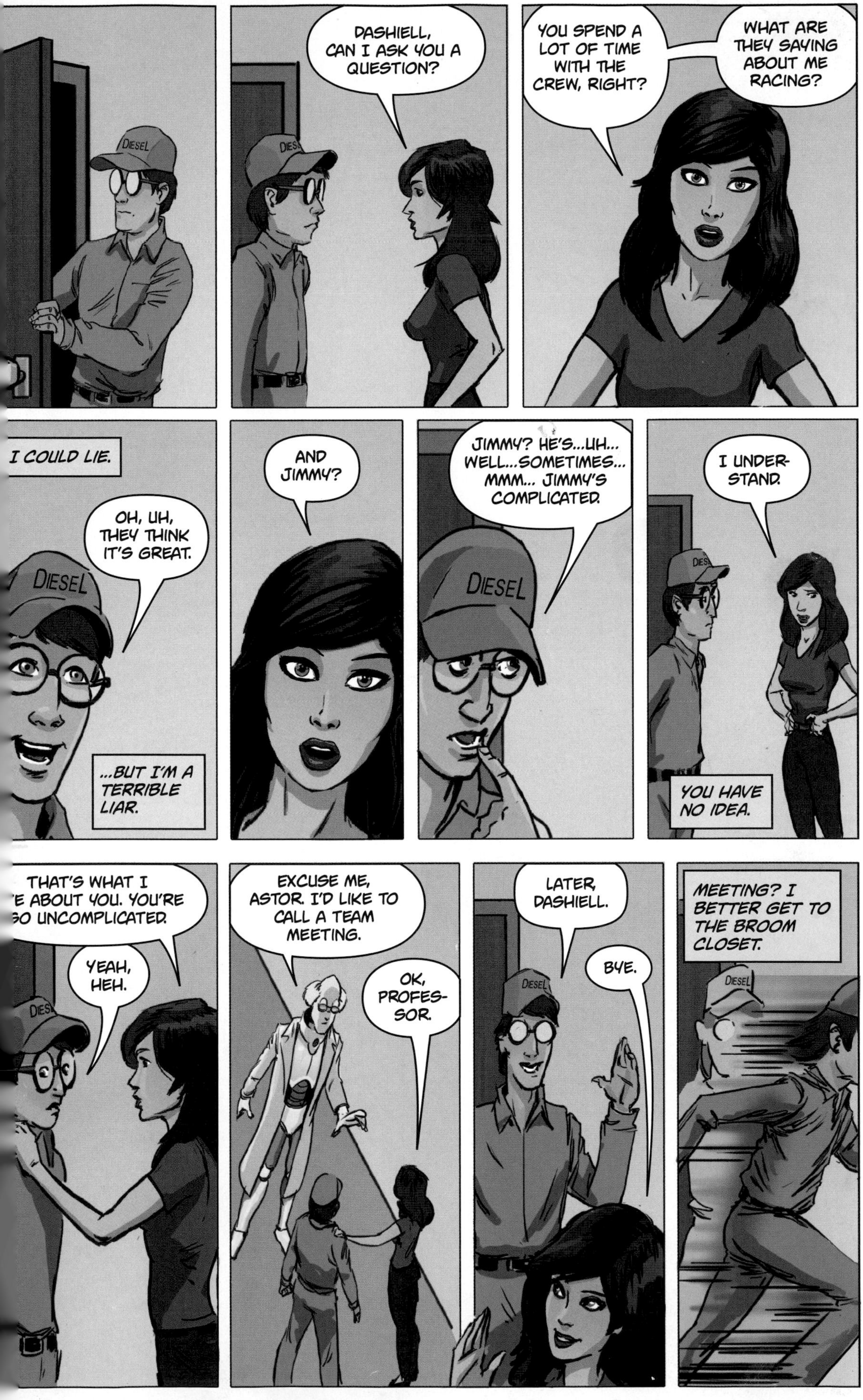
DASHIELL, CAN I ASK YOU A QUESTION?
YOU SPEND A LOT OF TIME WITH THE CREW, RIGHT?
WHAT ARE THEY SAYING ABOUT ME RACING?
I COULD LIE.
OH, UH, THEY THINK IT'S GREAT.
...BUT I'M A TERRIBLE LIAR.
AND JIMMY?
JIMMY? HE'S...UH... WELL...SOMETIMES... MMM... JIMMY'S COMPLICATED.
I UNDER-STAND.
YOU HAVE NO IDEA.
THAT'S WHAT I 'E ABOUT YOU. YOU'RE SO UNCOMPLICATED.
YEAH, HEH.
EXCUSE ME, ASTOR. I'D LIKE TO CALL A TEAM MEETING.
OK, PROFES-SOR.
LATER, DASHIELL.
BYE.
MEETING? I BETTER GET TO THE BROOM CLOSET.

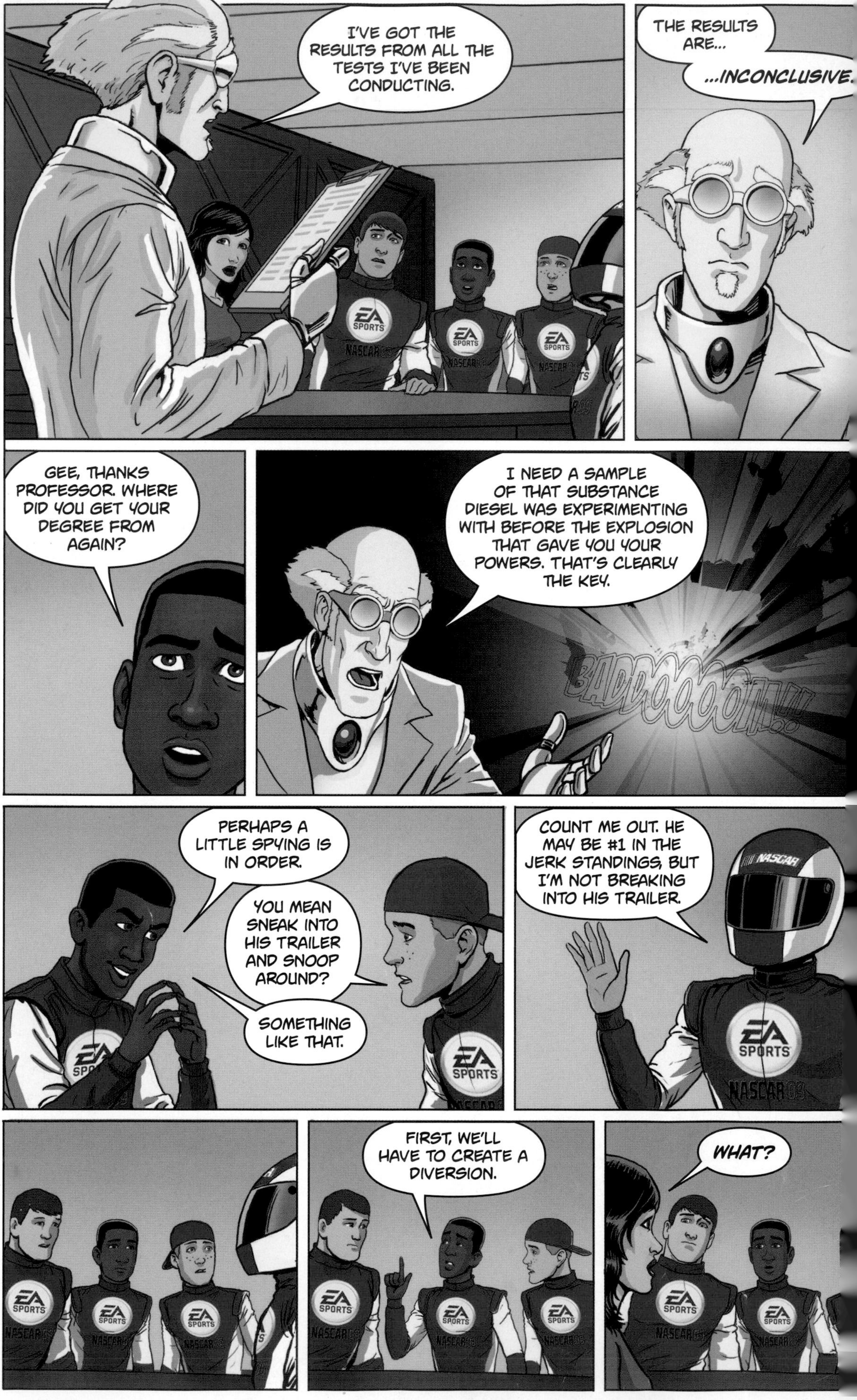

I'VE GOT THE RESULTS FROM ALL THE TESTS I'VE BEEN CONDUCTING.
THE RESULTS ARE...
...INCONCLUSIVE.
GEE, THANKS PROFESSOR. WHERE DID YOU GET YOUR DEGREE FROM AGAIN?
I NEED A SAMPLE OF THAT SUBSTANCE DIESEL WAS EXPERIMENTING WITH BEFORE THE EXPLOSION THAT GAVE YOU YOUR POWERS. THAT'S CLEARLY THE KEY.
PERHAPS A LITTLE SPYING IS IN ORDER.
YOU MEAN SNEAK INTO HIS TRAILER AND SNOOP AROUND?
SOMETHING LIKE THAT.
COUNT ME OUT. HE MAY BE #1 IN THE JERK STANDINGS, BUT I'M NOT BREAKING INTO HIS TRAILER.
FIRST, WE'LL HAVE TO CREATE A DIVERSION.
WHAT?

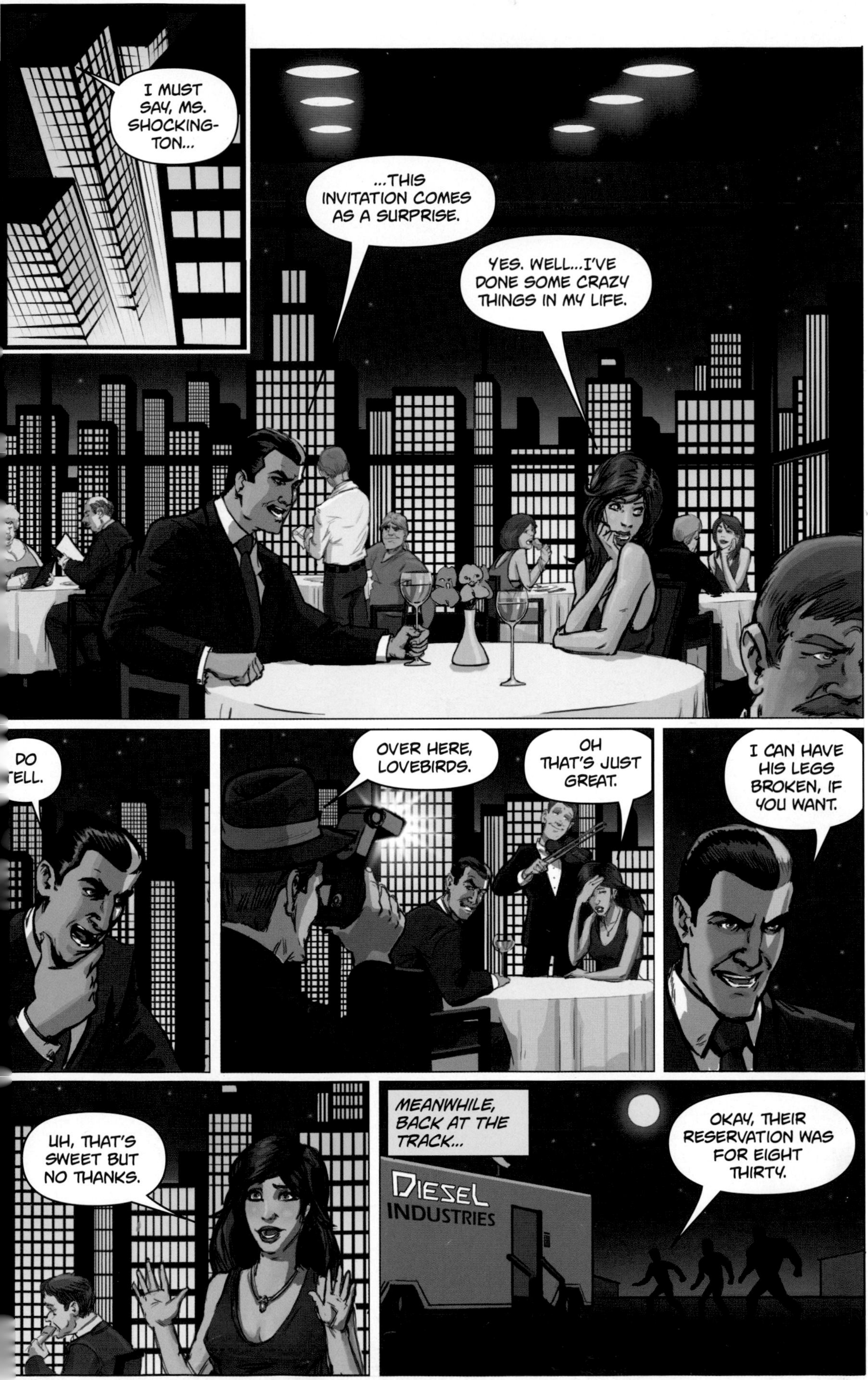
I MUST SAY, MS. SHOCKING-TON...
...THIS INVITATION COMES AS A SURPRISE.
YES. WELL...I'VE DONE SOME CRAZY THINGS IN MY LIFE.
DO TELL.
OVER HERE, LOVEBIRDS.
OH THAT'S JUST GREAT.
I CAN HAVE HIS LEGS BROKEN, IF YOU WANT.
UH, THAT'S SWEET BUT NO THANKS.
MEANWHILE, BACK AT THE TRACK...
DIESEL INDUSTRIES
OKAY, THEIR RESERVATION WAS FOR EIGHT THIRTY.

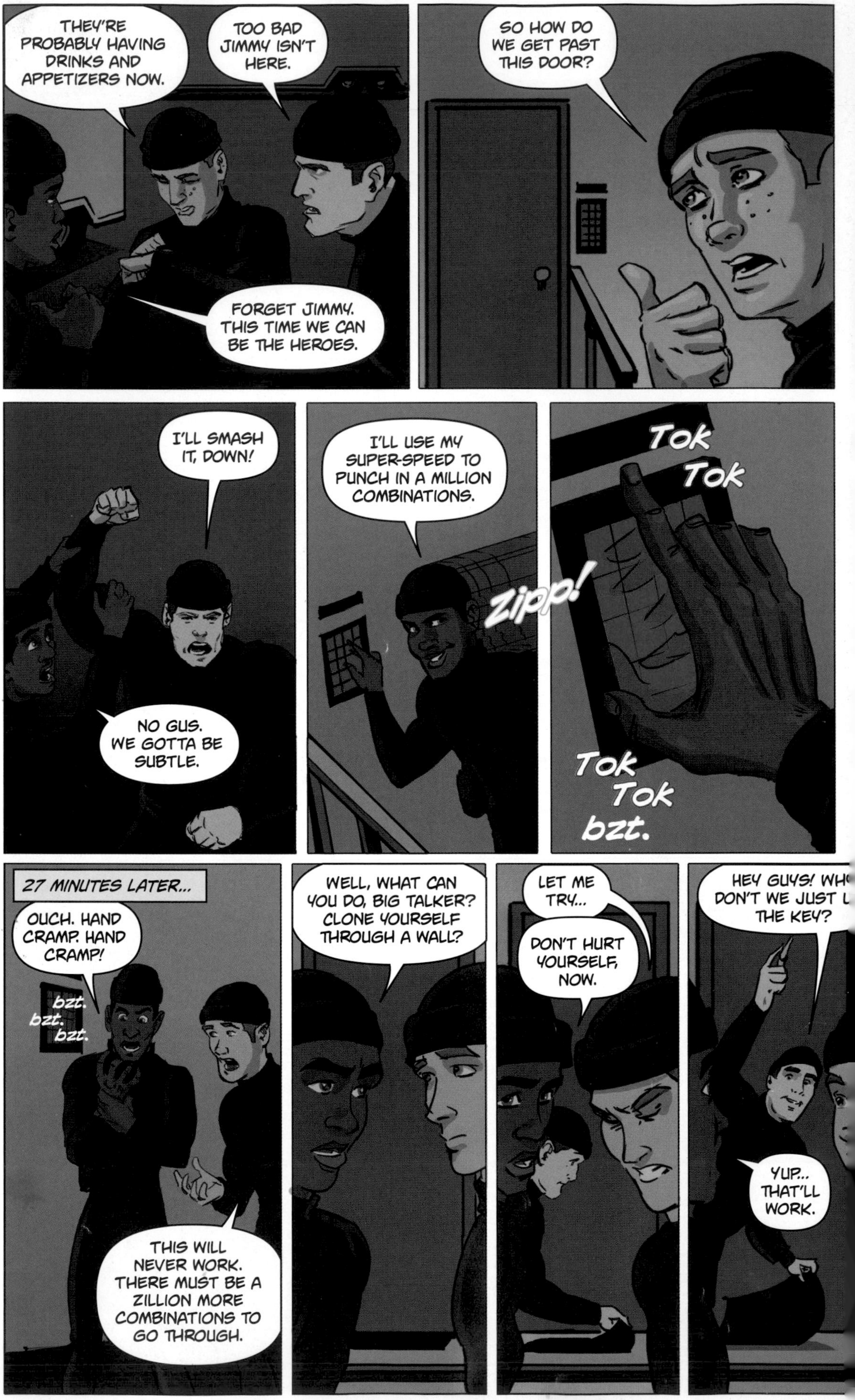
THEY'RE PROBABLY HAVING DRINKS AND APPETIZERS NOW.
TOO BAD JIMMY ISN'T HERE.
FORGET JIMMY. THIS TIME WE CAN BE THE HEROES.
SO HOW DO WE GET PAST THIS DOOR?
I'LL SMASH IT, DOWN!
NO GUS. WE GOTTA BE SUBTLE.
I'LL USE MY SUPER-SPEED TO PUNCH IN A MILLION COMBINATIONS.
ZIPP!
Tok
Tok
Tok
Tok
bzt.
27 MINUTES LATER...
OUCH. HAND CRAMP. HAND CRAMP!
bzt.
bzt.
bzt.
THIS WILL NEVER WORK. THERE MUST BE A ZILLION MORE COMBINATIONS TO GO THROUGH.
WELL, WHAT CAN YOU DO, BIG TALKER? CLONE YOURSELF THROUGH A WALL?
LET ME TRY...
DON'T HURT YOURSELF, NOW.
YUP... THAT'LL WORK.

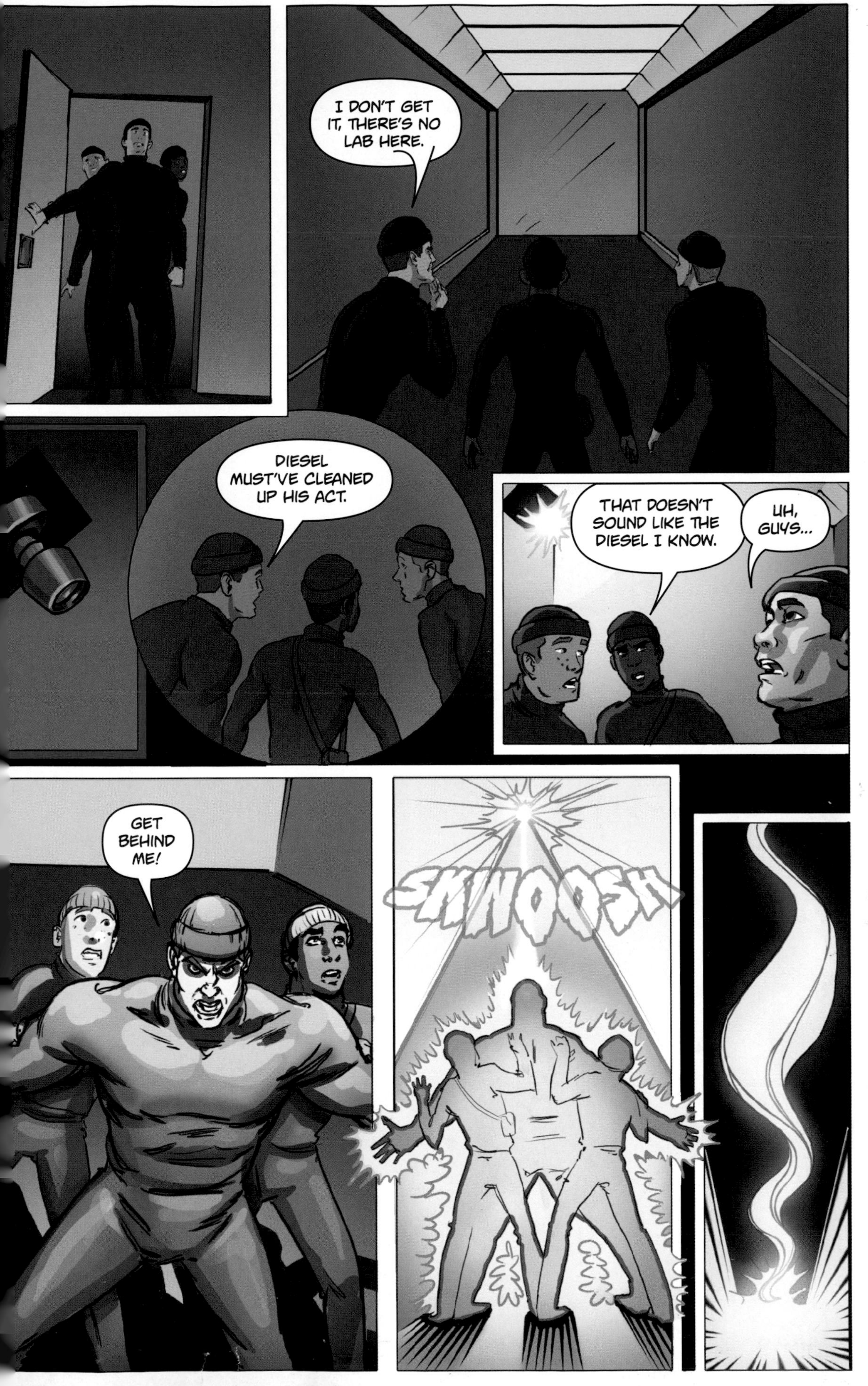

I DON'T GET IT, THERE'S NO LAB HERE.
DIESEL MUST'VE CLEANED UP HIS ACT.
THAT DOESN'T SOUND LIKE THE DIESEL I KNOW.
UH, GUYS...
GET BEHIND ME!
SKNOOSH

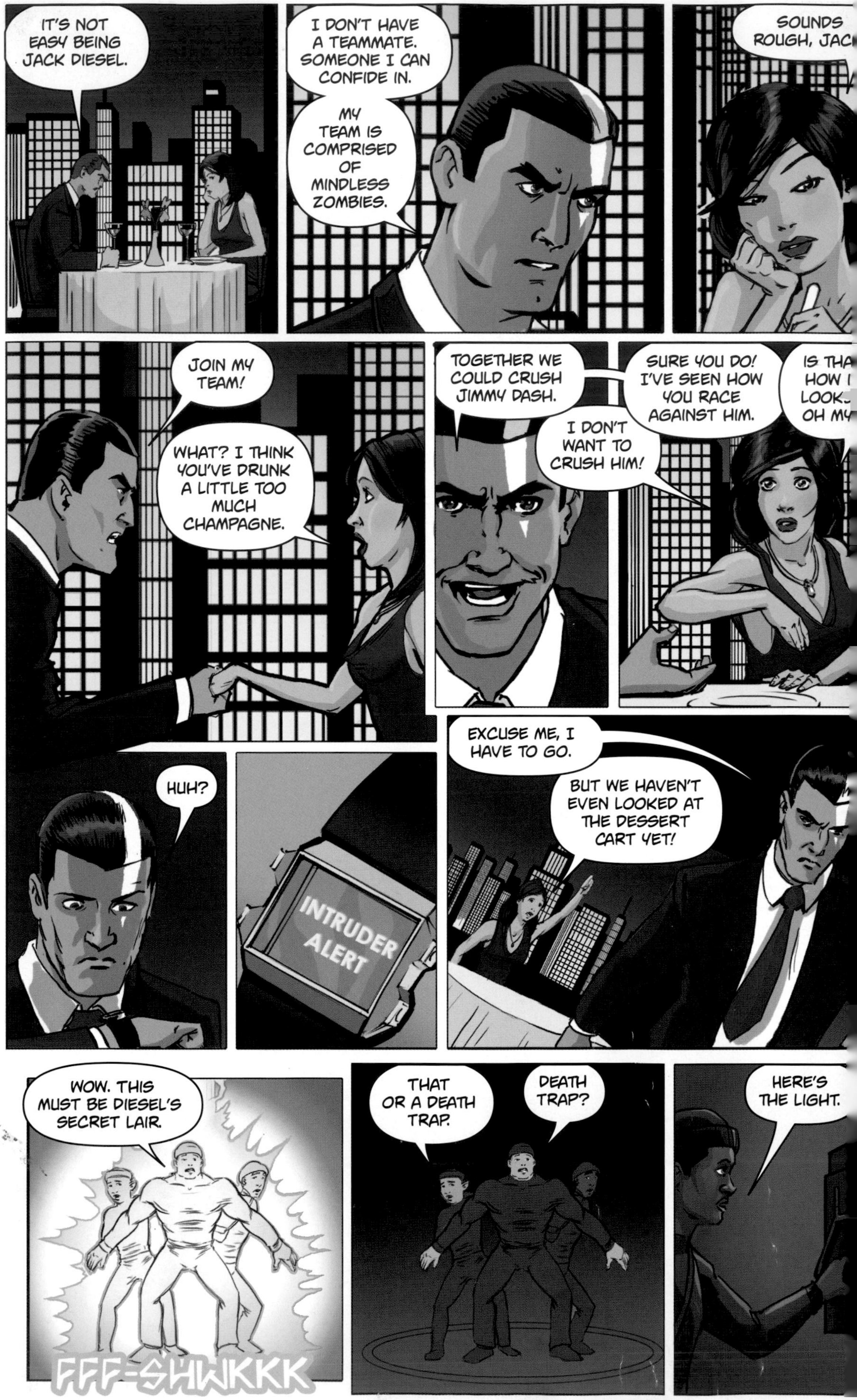
IT'S NOT EASY BEING JACK DIESEL.
I DON'T HAVE A TEAMMATE. SOMEONE I CAN CONFIDE IN.
MY TEAM IS COMPRISED OF MINDLESS ZOMBIES.
SOUNDS ROUGH, JAC
JOIN MY TEAM!
WHAT? I THINK YOU'VE DRUNK A LITTLE TOO MUCH CHAMPAGNE.
TOGETHER WE COULD CRUSH JIMMY DASH.
I DON'T WANT TO CRUSH HIM!
SURE YOU DO! I'VE SEEN HOW YOU RACE AGAINST HIM.
IS THA HOW I LOOK OH MY
HUH?
INTRUDER ALERT
EXCUSE ME, I HAVE TO GO.
BUT WE HAVEN'T EVEN LOOKED AT THE DESSERT CART YET!
WOW. THIS MUST BE DIESEL'S SECRET LAIR.
FFF-SHWKKK
THAT OR A DEATH TRAP.
DEATH TRAP?
HERE'S THE LIGHT.

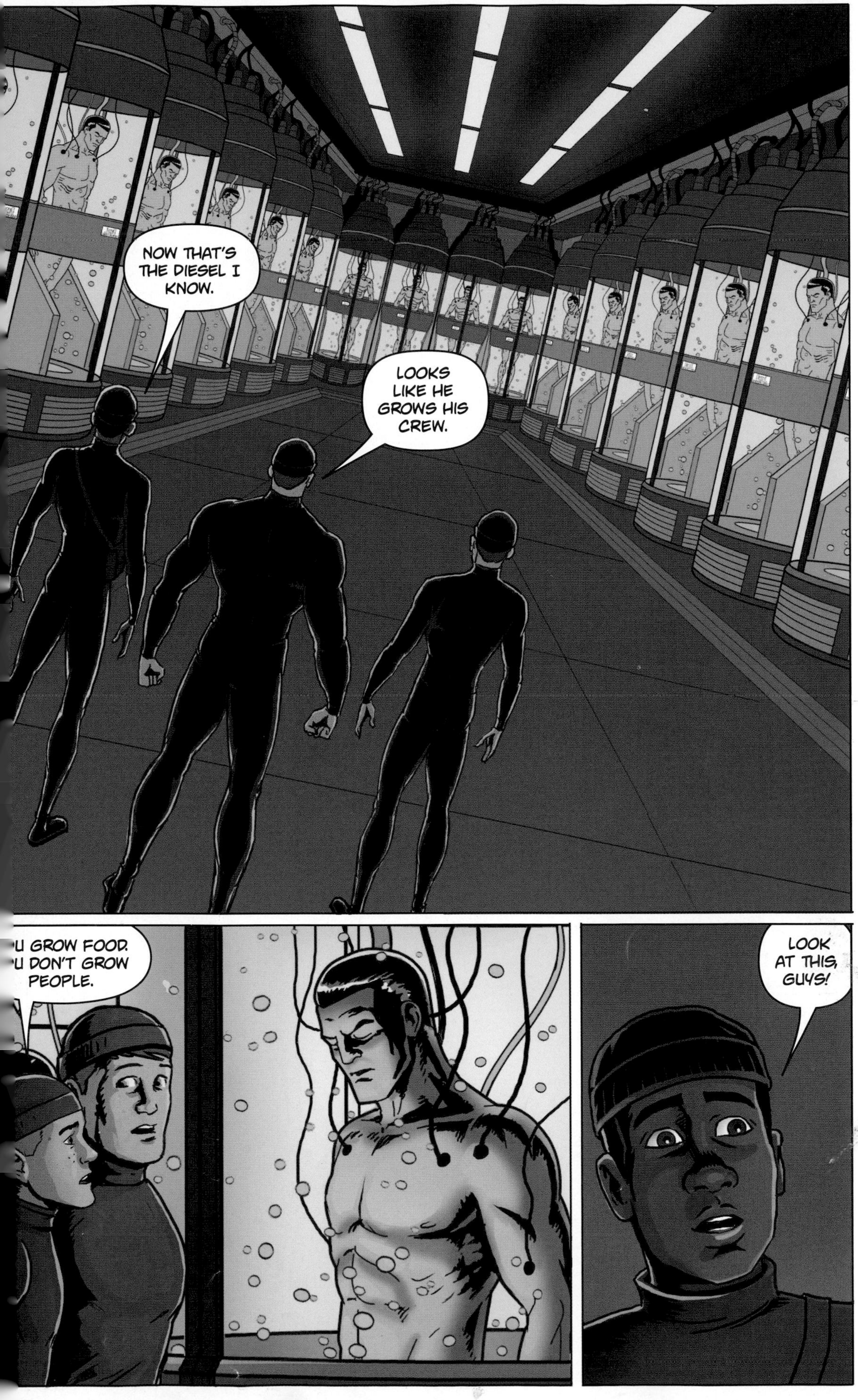
NOW THAT'S THE DIESEL I KNOW.
LOOKS LIKE HE GROWS HIS CREW.
U GROW FOOD. U DON'T GROW PEOPLE.
LOOK AT THIS, GUYS!

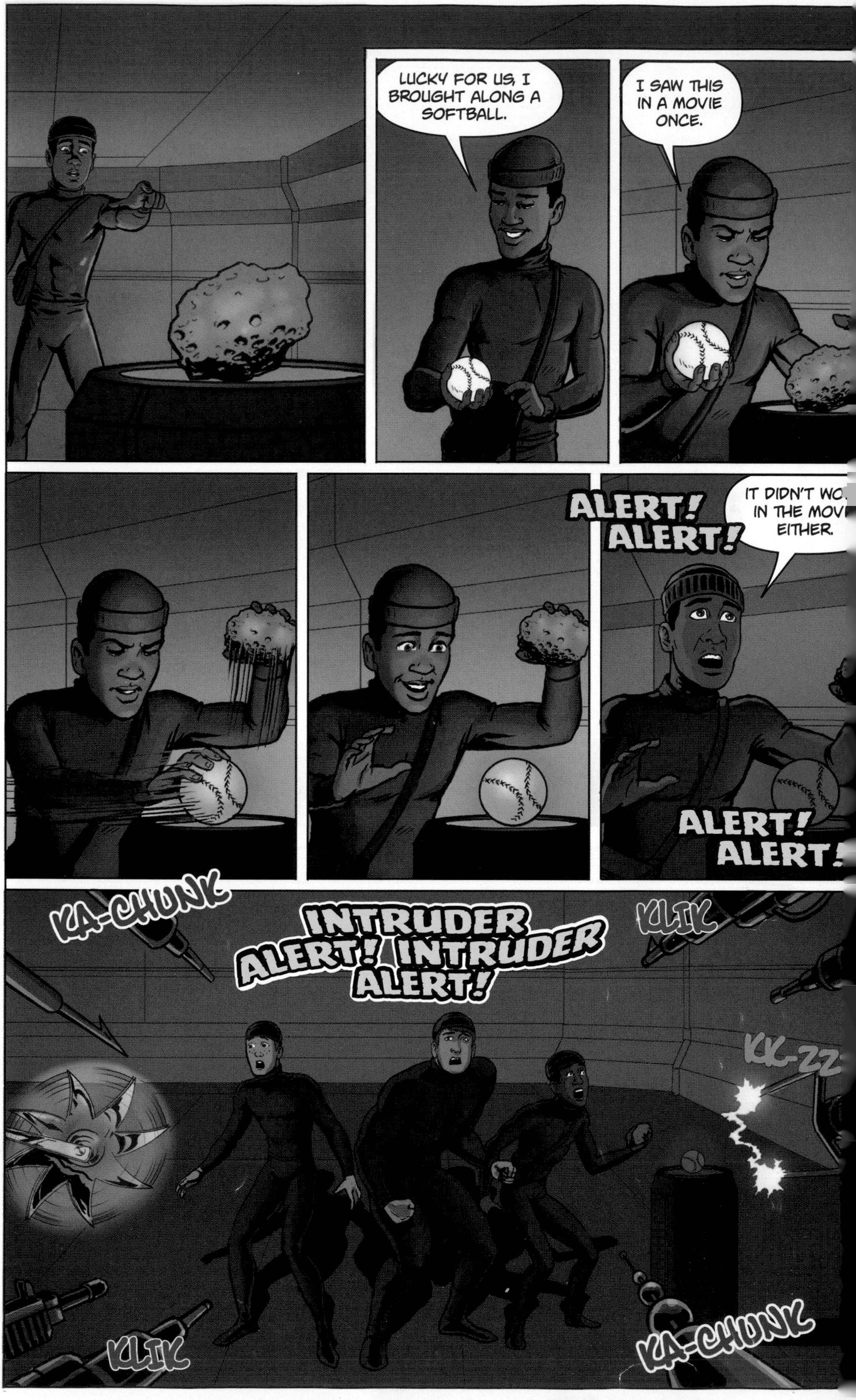

LUCKY FOR US, I BROUGHT ALONG A SOFTBALL.
I SAW THIS IN A MOVIE ONCE.
ALERT! ALERT!
IT DIDN'T WO IN THE MOVI EITHER.
ALERT! ALERT!
KA-CHUNK
INTRUDER ALERT! INTRUDER ALERT!
KLIK
KK-ZZ
KLIK
KA-CHUNK

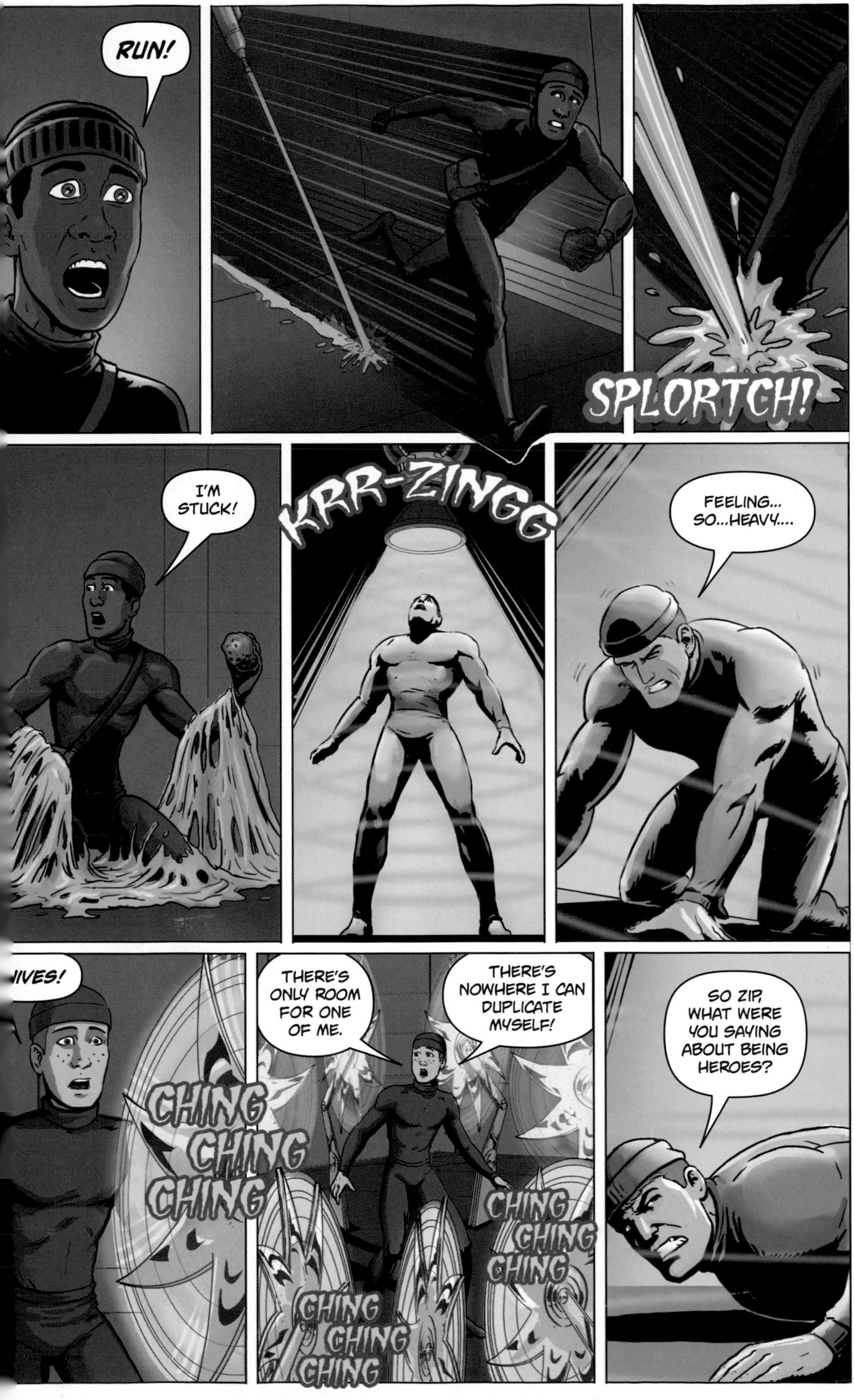
RUN!
SPLORTCH!
I'M STUCK!
KRR-ZINGG
FEELING... SO...HEAVY....
IVES!
CHING CHING CHING
THERE'S ONLY ROOM FOR ONE OF ME.
THERE'S NOWHERE I CAN DUPLICATE MYSELF!
CHING CHING CHING
CHING CHING CHING
SO ZIP, WHAT WERE YOU SAYING ABOUT BEING HEROES?

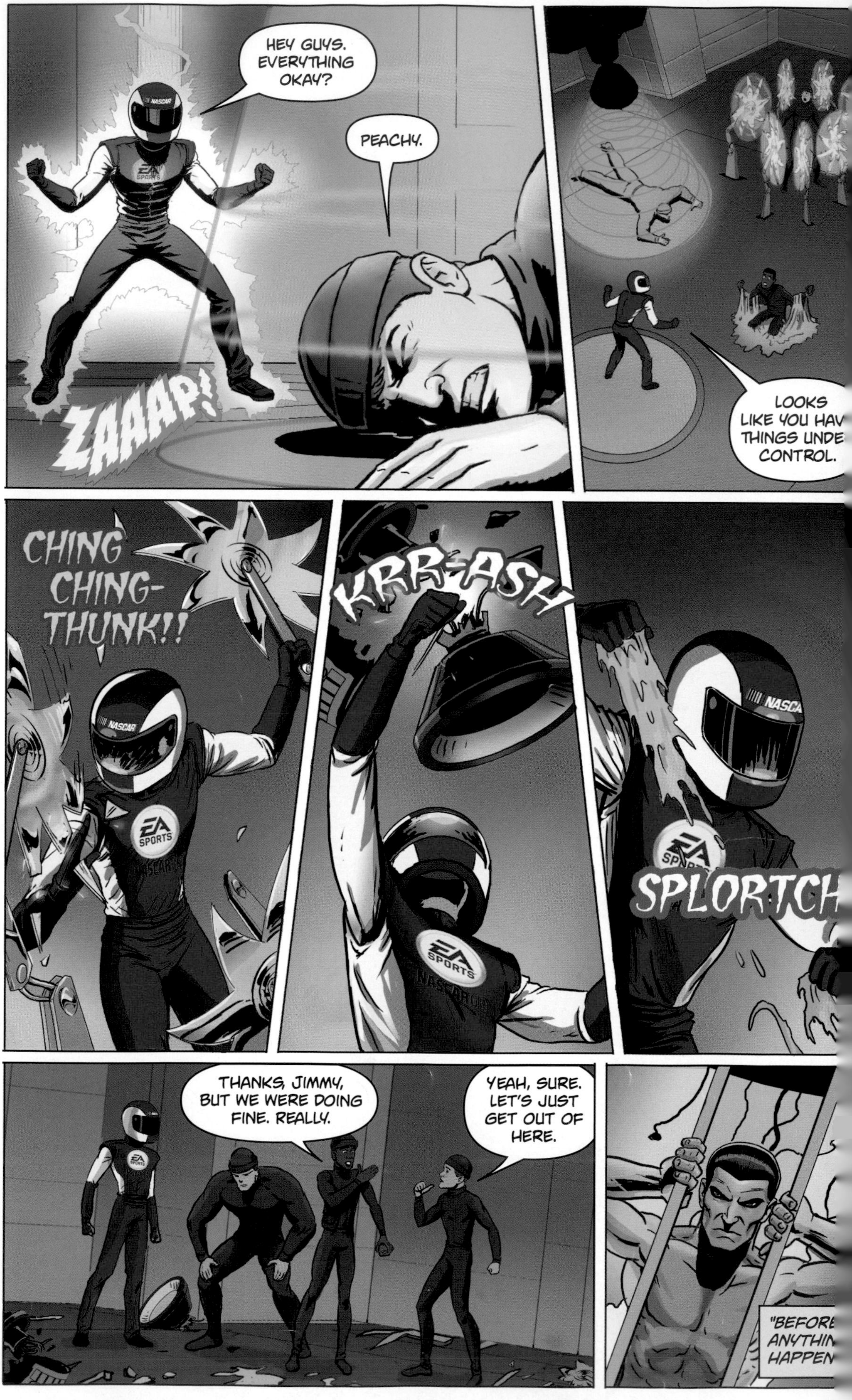
HEY GUYS. EVERYTHING OKAY?
PEACHY.
ZAAAP!
LOOKS LIKE YOU HAV THINGS UNDE CONTROL.
CHING CHING-THUNK!!
KRR-ASH
SPLORTCH
THANKS, JIMMY, BUT WE WERE DOING FINE. REALLY.
YEAH, SURE. LET'S JUST GET OUT OF HERE.
"BEFORE ANYTHIN HAPPEN

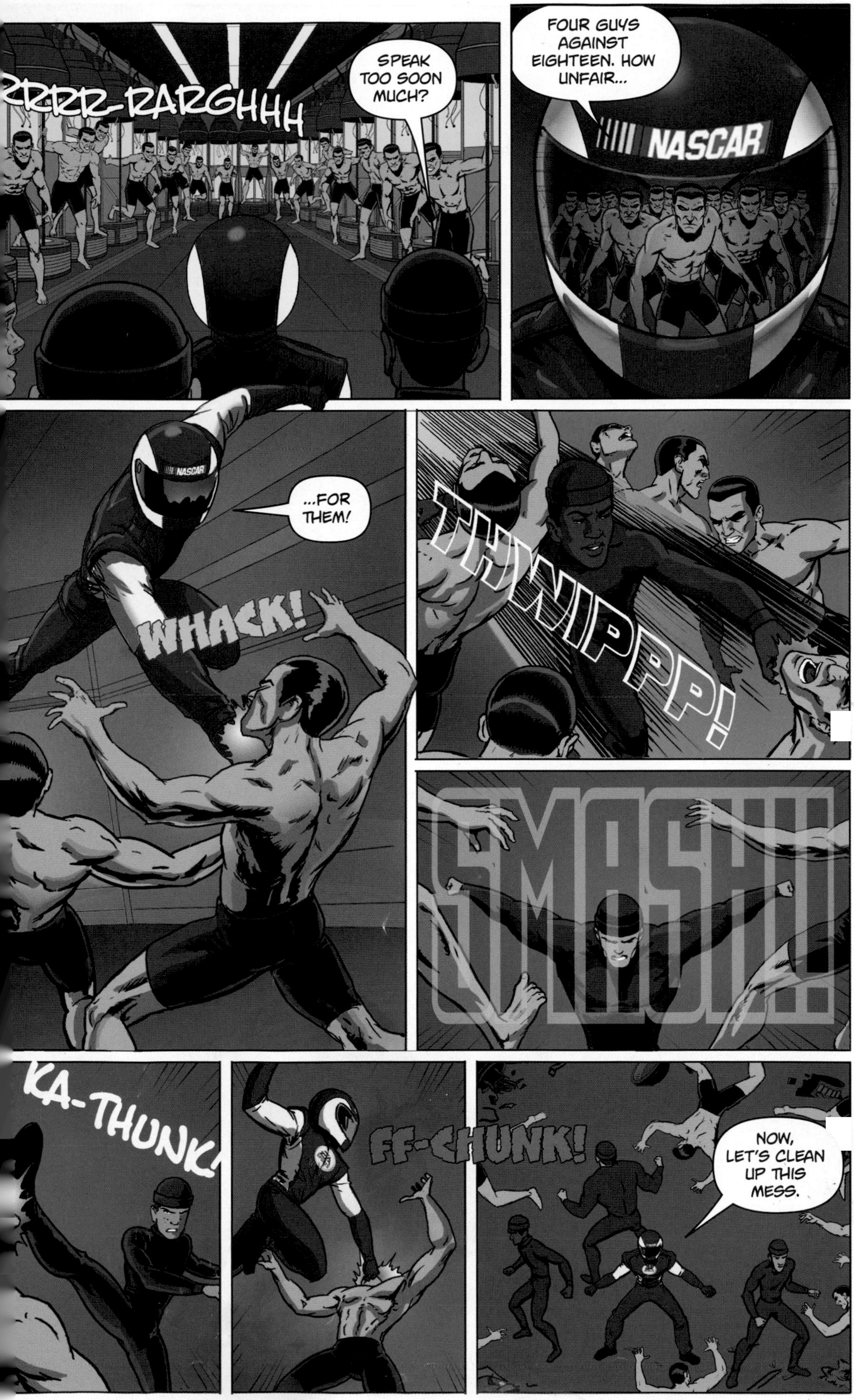

RRRR-RARGHHH
SPEAK TOO SOON MUCH?
FOUR GUYS AGAINST EIGHTEEN. HOW UNFAIR...
NASCAR
NASCAR
...FOR THEM!
WHACK!
THWIPPP!
SMASH!!
KA-THUNK!
FF-CHUNK!
NOW, LET'S CLEAN UP THIS MESS.

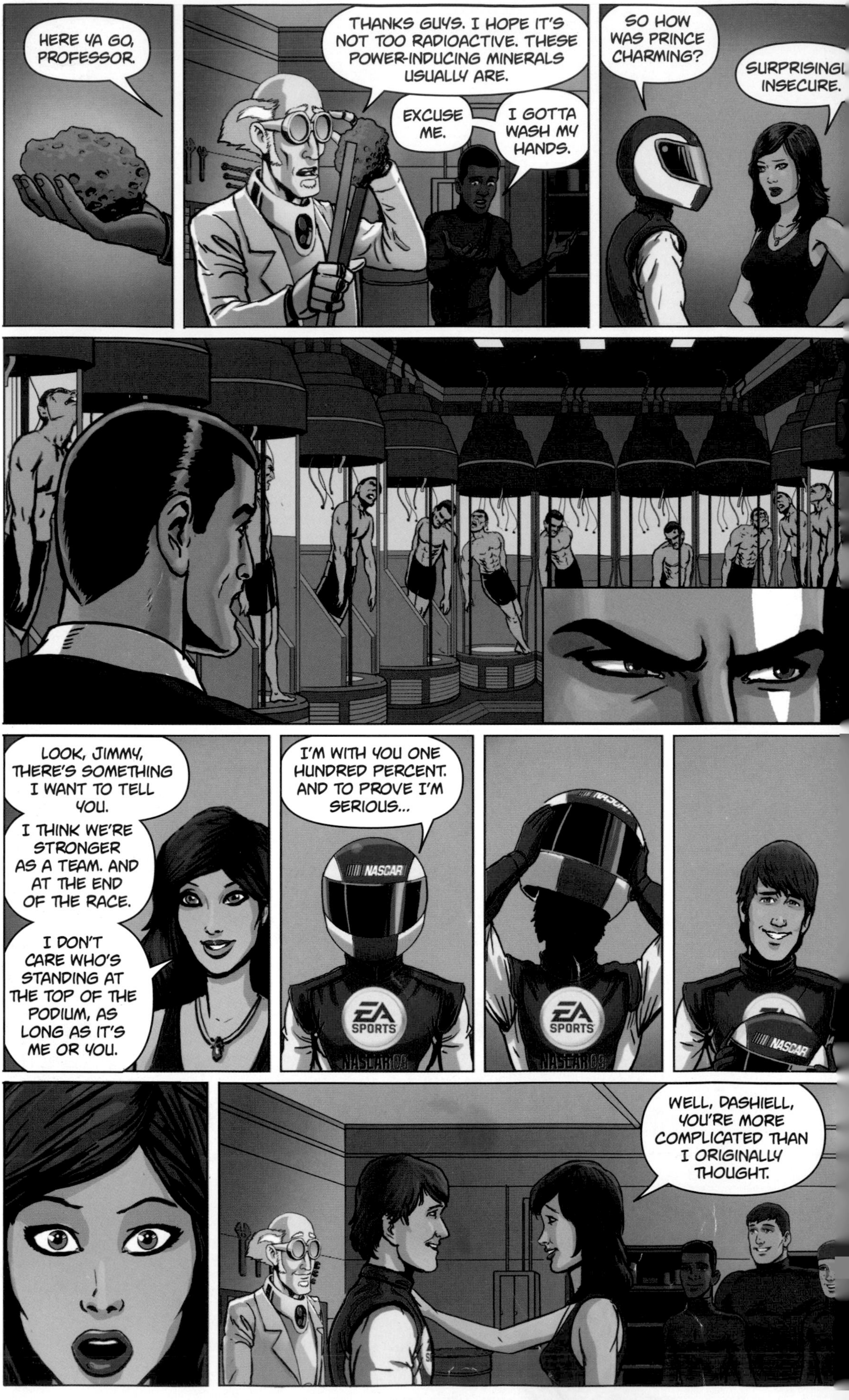
HERE YA GO, PROFESSOR.
THANKS GUYS. I HOPE IT'S NOT TOO RADIOACTIVE. THESE POWER-INDUCING MINERALS USUALLY ARE.
EXCUSE ME.
I GOTTA WASH MY HANDS.
SO HOW WAS PRINCE CHARMING?
SURPRISINGL INSECURE.
LOOK, JIMMY, THERE'S SOMETHING I WANT TO TELL YOU.
I THINK WE'RE STRONGER AS A TEAM. AND AT THE END OF THE RACE.
I DON'T CARE WHO'S STANDING AT THE TOP OF THE PODIUM, AS LONG AS IT'S ME OR YOU.
I'M WITH YOU ONE HUNDRED PERCENT. AND TO PROVE I'M SERIOUS...
NASCAR
EA SPORTS
NASCAR 08
WELL, DASHIELL, YOU'RE MORE COMPLICATED THAN I ORIGINALLY THOUGHT.

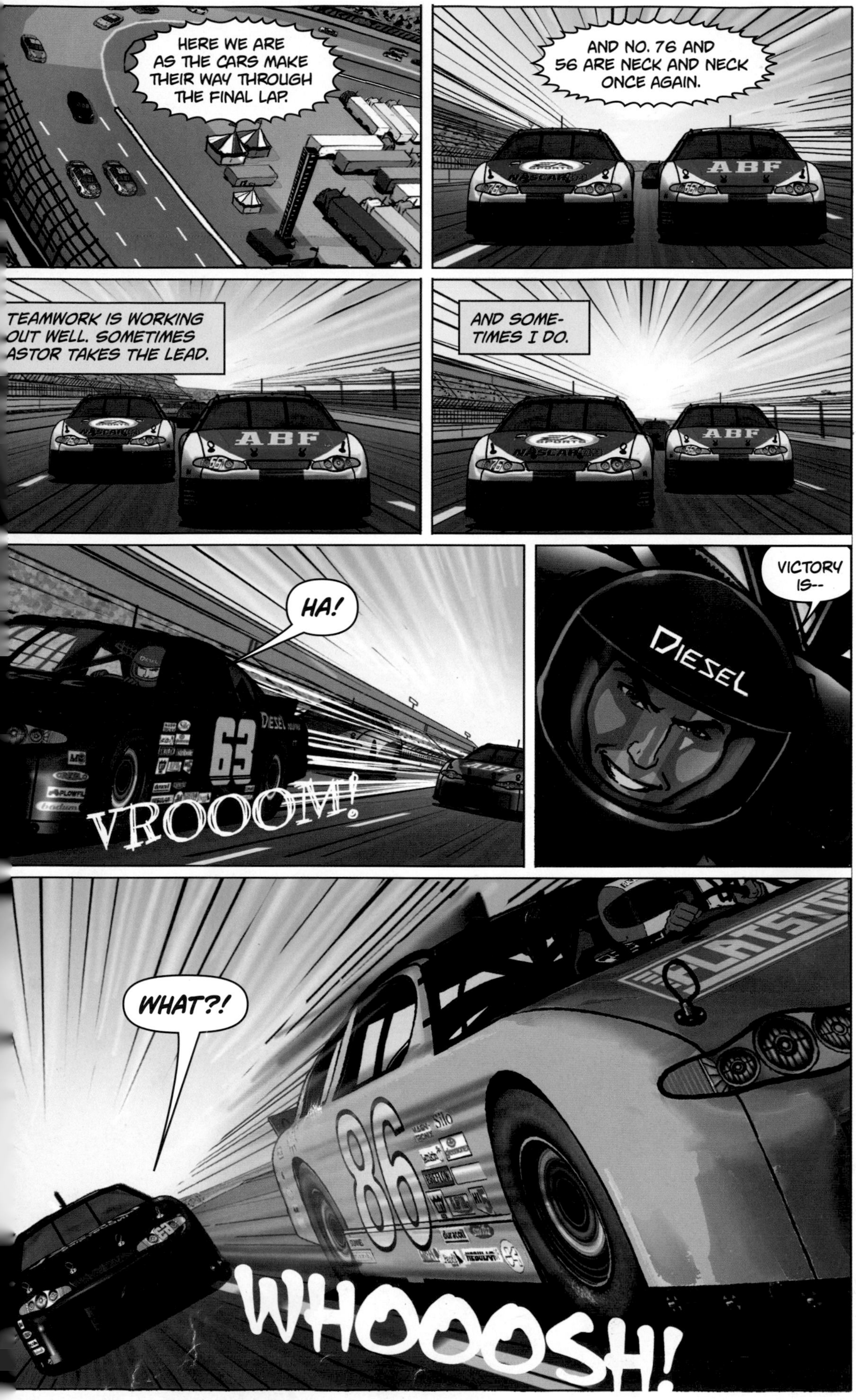
HERE WE ARE AS THE CARS MAKE THEIR WAY THROUGH THE FINAL LAP.
AND NO. 76 AND 56 ARE NECK AND NECK ONCE AGAIN.
TEAMWORK IS WORKING OUT WELL. SOMETIMES ASTOR TAKES THE LEAD.
AND SOME-TIMES I DO.
HA!
VROOOM!
VICTORY IS--
DIESEL
WHAT?!
WHOOOSH!

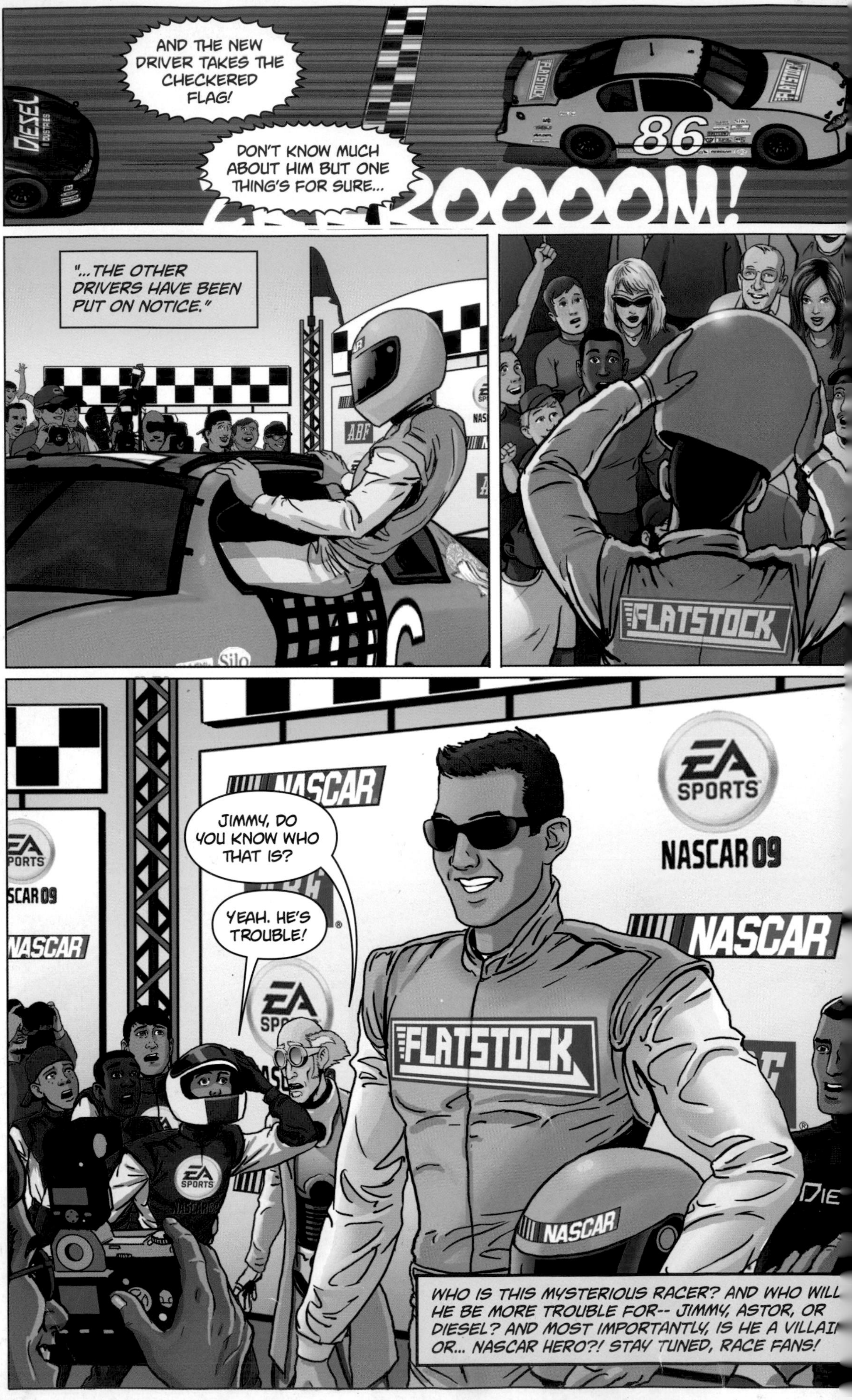

AND THE NEW DRIVER TAKES THE CHECKERED FLAG!
DON'T KNOW MUCH ABOUT HIM BUT ONE THING'S FOR SURE...
DIESEL
FLATSTOCK
86
ROOOOM!
"...THE OTHER DRIVERS HAVE BEEN PUT ON NOTICE."
ABF
FLATSTOCK
NASCAR
EA SPORTS
NASCAR 09
JIMMY, DO YOU KNOW WHO THAT IS?
YEAH. HE'S TROUBLE!
NASCAR
FLATSTOCK
NASCAR
WHO IS THIS MYSTERIOUS RACER? AND WHO WILL HE BE MORE TROUBLE FOR-- JIMMY, ASTOR, OR DIESEL? AND MOST IMPORTANTLY, IS HE A VILLAIN OR... NASCAR HERO?! STAY TUNED, RACE FANS!

NASCAR HEROES

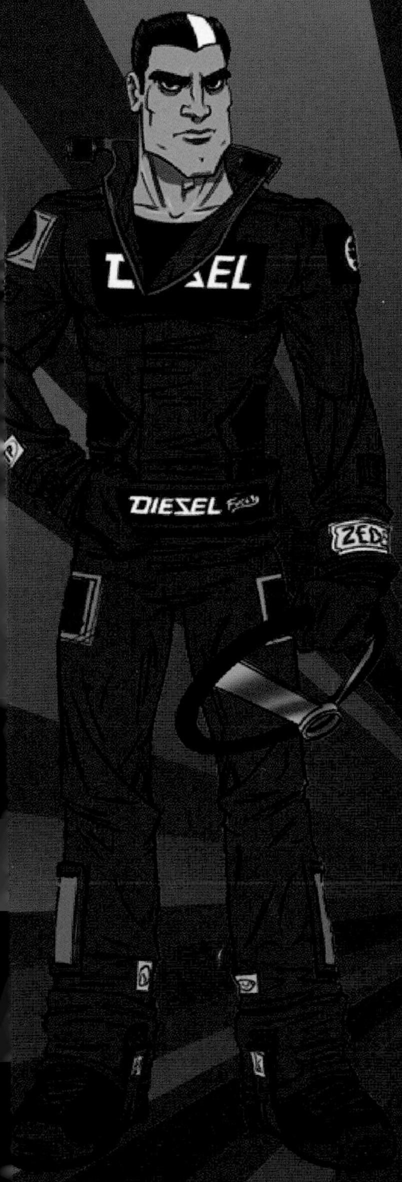
DIESEL
DIESEL

JACK DIESEL

WE KNOW THAT THE INFAMOUS NASCAR DRIVER JACK DIESEL ALWAYS SEEMS TO BE AT THE TOP OF THE POINTS STANDINGS. WHAT WE DON'T KNOW IS HOW HE DOES IT. WITH THE EMERGENCE OF HOT-SHOT ROOKIE CHALLENGER JIMMY DASH ON THE SCENE, WILL DIESEL BE EXPOSED?

JACK DIESEL

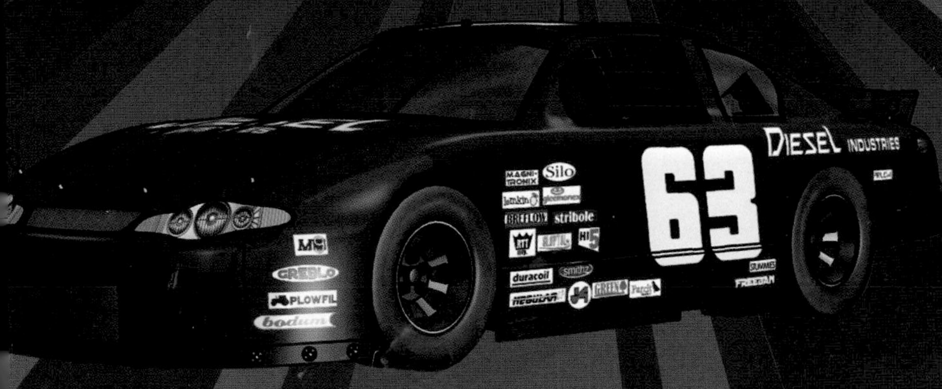
DIESEL INDUSTRIES
63
Silo
stribole
duracoil
GREBLO
PLOWFIL
bodum

NASCAR HEROES

ASTOR SHOCKINGTON A.K.A SHOQUE

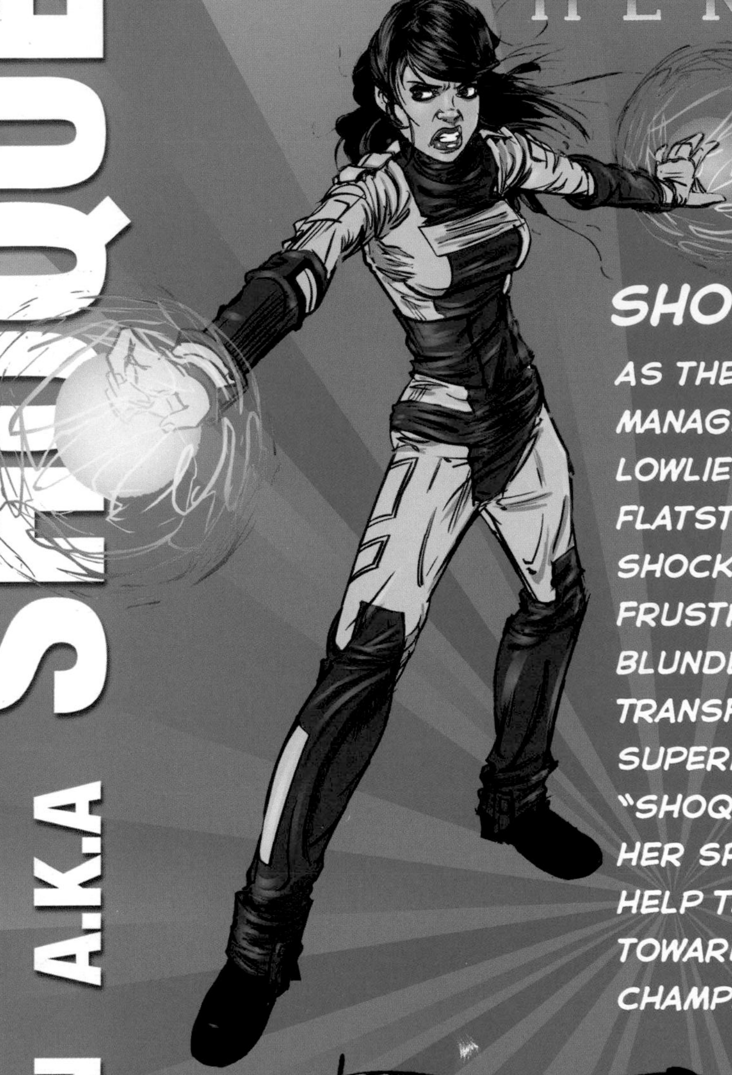

ASTOR SHOCKINGTON

AS THE OPERATIONS MANAGER OF NASCAR'S LOWLIEST RACING TEAM, FLATSTOCK, MS. ASTOR SHOCKINGTON IS FRUSTRATED BY HER BLUNDERING CREW. TRANSFORMED INTO SUPERHEROINE "SHOQUE," SHE USES HER SPECIAL POWERS TO HELP TEAM FLATSTOCK TOWARDS A TEAM CHAMPIONSHIP.

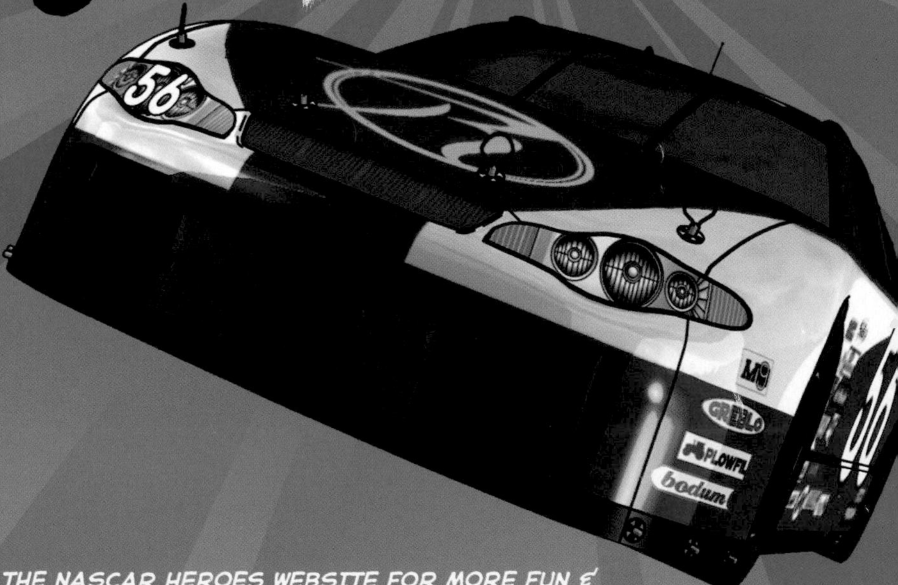
56
bodum

HOW TO DRAW
JIMMY DASH

NASCAR COMICS

BY JOHN GALLAGHER

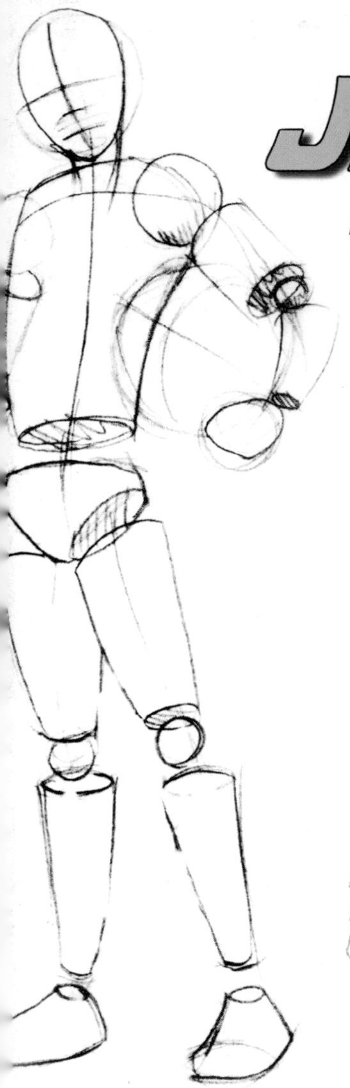

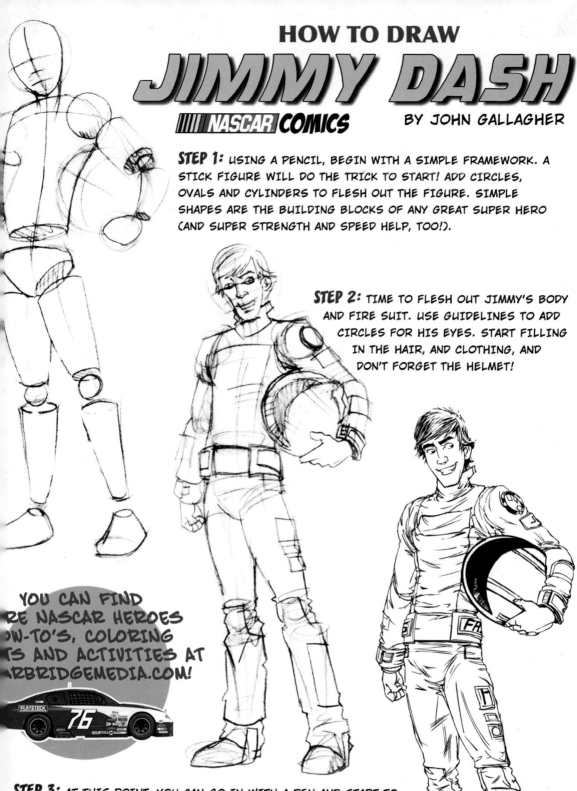

STEP 1: USING A PENCIL, BEGIN WITH A SIMPLE FRAMEWORK. A STICK FIGURE WILL DO THE TRICK TO START! ADD CIRCLES, OVALS AND CYLINDERS TO FLESH OUT THE FIGURE. SIMPLE SHAPES ARE THE BUILDING BLOCKS OF ANY GREAT SUPER HERO (AND SUPER STRENGTH AND SPEED HELP, TOO!).

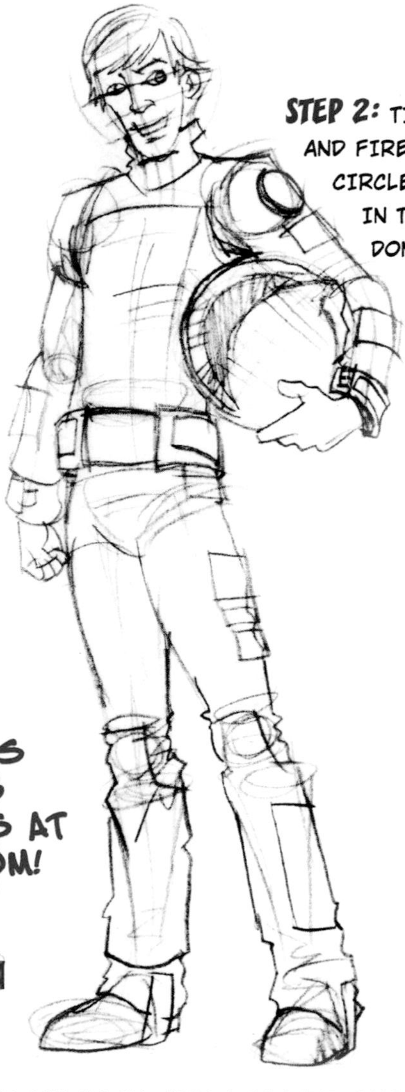

STEP 2: TIME TO FLESH OUT JIMMY'S BODY AND FIRE SUIT. USE GUIDELINES TO ADD CIRCLES FOR HIS EYES. START FILLING IN THE HAIR, AND CLOTHING, AND DON'T FORGET THE HELMET!

YOU CAN FIND
RE NASCAR HEROES
W-TO'S, COLORING
TS AND ACTIVITIES AT
RBRIDGEMEDIA.COM!

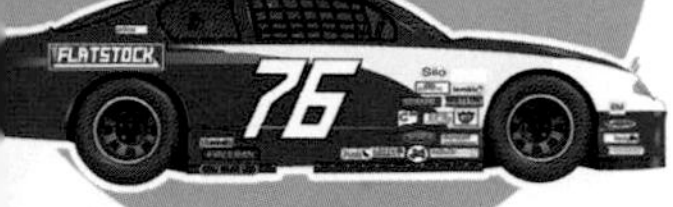
FLATSTOCK
76

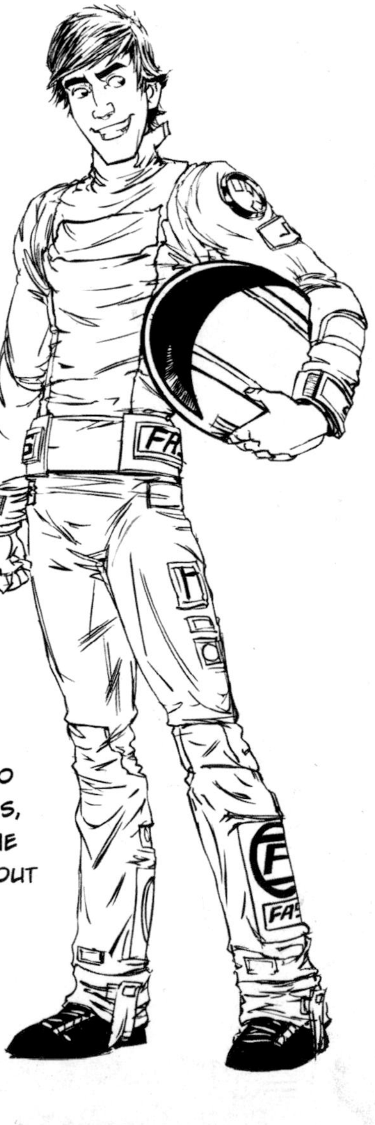

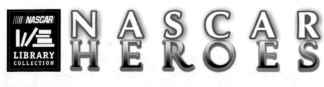

STEP 3: AT THIS POINT, YOU CAN GO IN WITH A PEN AND START TO INK THE FIGURE. ERASE THE PENCIL LINES UNDERNEATH THE INKS, FIXING ANY MISTAKES IN YOUR DRAWINGS. REMEMBER TO LET THE PEN INK DRY BEFORE ERASING, TO AVOID SMUDGES! NOW, PULL OUT YOUR MARKERS OR CRAYONS, AND ADD SOME COLOR!

NASCAR LIBRARY COLLECTION

NASCAR HEROES

HOW TO DRAW NASCAR COMICS

JACK DIESEL'S NO. 6

BY JOHN GALLAGHER

SURE, JACK DIESEL'S A BAD GUY, BUT HE'S GOT A SET OF WHEELS THAT MAKE HIM A NASCAR SUPERSTAR! HERE'S A QUICK GUIDE ON HOW YOU CAN DRAW JACK'S RIDE!

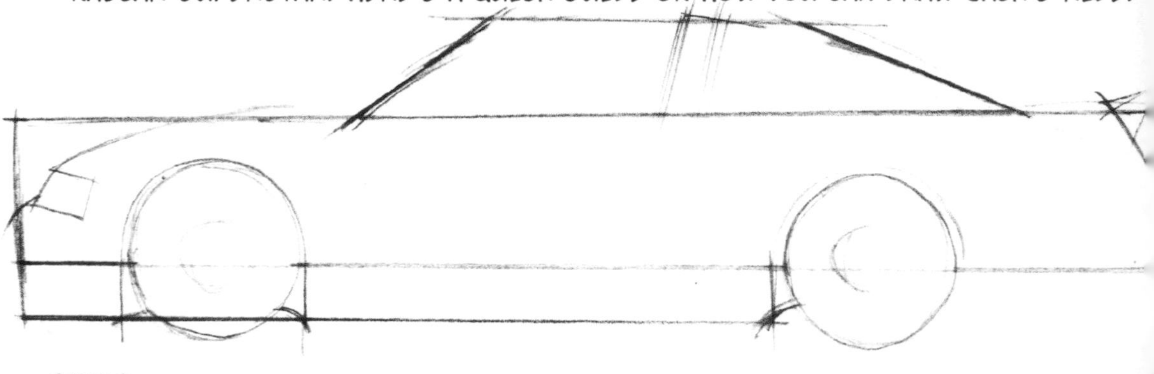

STEP 1: START OFF BY DRAWING A SERIES OF BOXES, SUGGESTING THE SHAPE OF THE CAR AND TIRES. IT'S LIKE CREATING A SHAPE WITH BUILDING BLOCKS, THEN CARVING AWAY AT THE SHAP INSIDE. YOU CAN DO THIS FREEHAND, OR WITH A RULER, DEPENDING ON HOW "TIGHT" YOU WANT YOUR DRAWING!

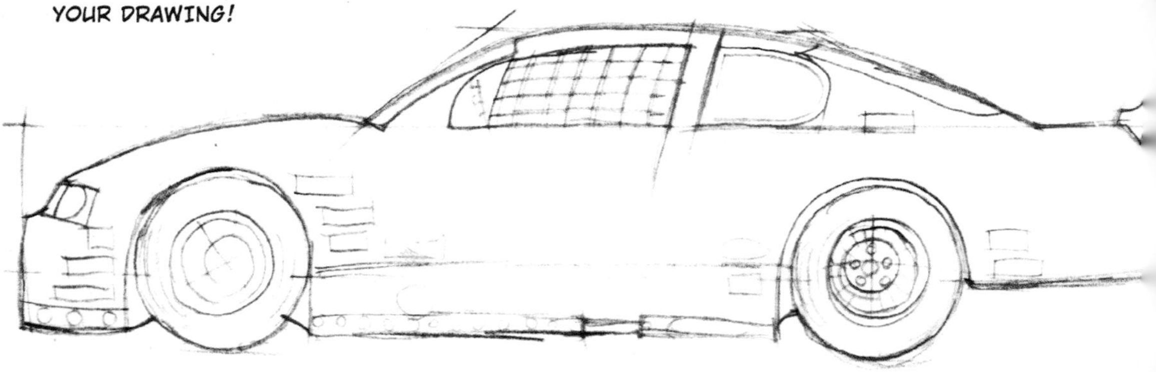

STEP 2: NOW, START TO ZERO IN ON THE SHAPE OF THE CAR FRONT, WINDOWS, TIRES, AND REA SPOILER. THEN, YOU'LL WANT TO ADD THE DETAILS THAT MAKE A NASCAR UNIQUE, LIKE DECALS, NUMBERS, AND RIVETS!

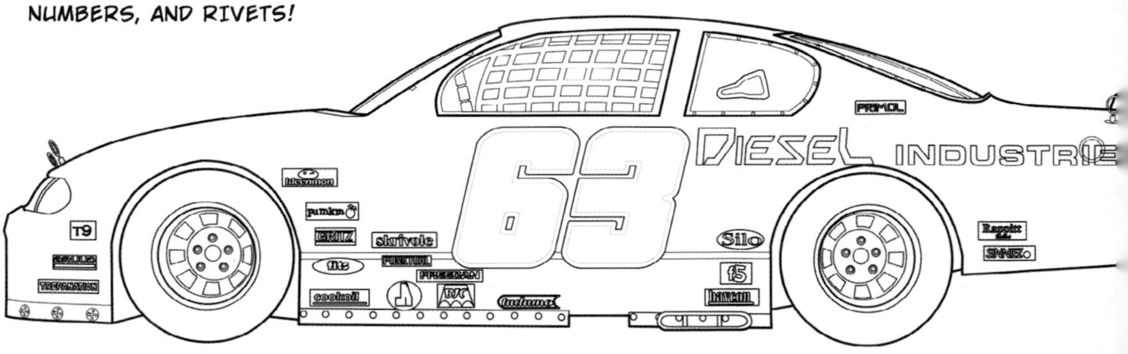
63
DIESEL
INDUSTRIE
PRIMOL
T9
Silo
f5
skrivole
cookoil

STEP 3: AT THIS POINT, YOU CAN GO IN WITH A PEN AND START TO INK THE CAR, REALLY SHARPE ING THE IMAGE! ERASE THE PENCIL LINES UNDERNEATH THE INKS, FIXING ANY MISTAKES IN YO DRAWING. GIVE THE CAR THE NUMBER OF YOUR FAVORITE DRIVE (BUT DON'T TELL JACK!), AND A SOME COLOR! NOW YOUR DRAWING IS READY TO RACE!

NASCAR LIBRARY COLLECTION

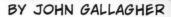

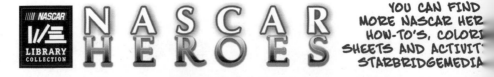

NASCAR HEROES

YOU CAN FIND MORE NASCAR HER HOW-TO'S, COLORI SHEETS AND ACTIVIT STARBRIDGEMEDIA